## "I bless the day you hired me."

"Do you?" Drew's eyes moved over her.

Eve nearly knocked over her wineglass at the look he gave her.

"Something about me still troubles you," he said.

"I don't think it wise to get personal."

He saw the guardedness that entered her face. "Except we're human. And Evie, though I know it's the last thing you want, we're attracted to each other."

Suddenly it was out. The secret that ran deep.

"I have a bit of a problem with breaking the rules."

"I can see that." Drew gave her a half smile. "Is having dinner with your boss breaking the rules?"

## From boardroom...to bride and groom!

Dear Reader,

Welcome to the second book in our MARRYING THE BOSS miniseries. *Boardroom Proposal* by Margaret Way is her 75th novel with Harlequin Romance.®

Over the following months, some of your favorite Harlequin Romance authors will be bringing you a variety of tantalizing stories about love in the workplace!

Falling for the boss can mean trouble, so our gorgeous heroes and lively heroines all struggle to resist their feelings of attraction for each other. But somehow love always ends up top of the agenda. And it isn't just a nine-to-five affair.... Mixing business with pleasure carries on after hours—and ends in marriage!

Happy Reading!

*The Editors*

Look out next month for a further novel in our
MARRYING THE BOSS series:
*Temporary Engagement* by Jessica Hart
Harlequin Romance #3544

# Margaret Way
## Boardroom Proposal

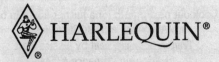

TORONTO • NEW YORK • LONDON
AMSTERDAM • PARIS • SYDNEY • HAMBURG
STOCKHOLM • ATHENS • TOKYO • MILAN • MADRID
PRAGUE • WARSAW • BUDAPEST • AUCKLAND

ISBN 0-373-03540-3

BOARDROOM PROPOSAL

First North American Publication 1999.

**Printed in U.S.A.**

# CHAPTER ONE

IT TOOK Eve exactly ten minutes to walk from Pearce Musgrave, the merchant bank where she worked, to the new Trans Continental Resources building two streets away in the swish riverside business precinct. She was only a few yards from the entrance when the city hall clock boomed the hour: 1:00 p.m. Right on schedule. Never one to leave anything to chance, she wanted time to cool down and get her thoughts together for the interview ahead. Subtropical Brisbane was in the grip of a heatwave; searing blue skies, steamy air, heat shimmering off the crowded lunchtime streets in quicksilver waves, giving the odd illusion one was walking through pools of water. But the moment she walked through TCR's automated glass doors, imprinted with the silver and blue interlocking rings of their logo, a current of cold air hit her.

It felt marvellous. She drew in a grateful breath, looking around the handsome expanse of the foyer with interest. This was TCR's new building replacing their old headquarters of many years. An ultra-modern glass tower, that late afternoon when the rays of the sun hit it, turned into a blazing column of light. Eve had witnessed the spectacle many times. It also announced to the business sector and the public at large Trans Continental Resources, mines, minerals, natural gas exploration, was one of the top corporations in the country and one of the few that allowed women power and authority. The high-profile Meg Topham held the position

5

of vice-chairman, so promotions were on merit and not on the old boy's network. An enormous incentive for Eve, who was determined on a successful career.

At twenty-four, Eve had long since made the decision marriage was not a top priority, although she had played bridesmaid to her girlfriends several times over. Marriage was for the wide-eyed romantics, the super-optimists, women with a history of family love and stability who didn't know about treachery and betrayal. There were other women not so fortunate. Women who were capable of dying when love was withdrawn from them. Eve had learned that to her sorrow. Love didn't always go hand in hand with happiness. The father she had thought herself so close to had broken their mother's heart when Eve was thirteen and her brother, Ben, just nine. Brad Copeland had simply come home one night and told his stunned wife, ''I want out, Maureen. I regret hurting you most terribly, but I've fallen in love.'' The timing had been especially good. Two weeks before Christmas.

Another woman. Some teenage seductress in his office. Anyway, someone less than half his age. ''I *need* her,'' he had cried emotionally, avoiding his wife's stricken eyes. ''I can't live without her. Our marriage is on the rocks anyway.'' A point of view so horribly new, it had overwhelmed their mother. Amazingly she had thought they were all held together by love. Love for each other. Love for their children.

While their father expounded on the hitherto unimagined rapture that had come into his life and their mother sobbed pitifully, Eve and Ben sat huddled together on the stairs, Ben crying broken-heartedly within the shelter of his big sister's arms, Eve so angry she felt alight. She had gone all her short life thinking her family was indestructible. Her parents loved each other. Sure they had their fights, but there were plenty of good times.

Now upheaval and desolation. And all over leaping male hormones. Lust wasn't love. It was a dark fantasy.

Memories, one after the other, crowded in, clamouring for attention. She remembered flying down the steps, pummelling her father, calling him every terrible name she could think of and, unlike Ben, she had always been able to articulate her feelings. She remembered her father had difficulty staving her off, hypocrite that he was with tears in his eyes. "I'm sorry, Evie, I'm sorry. God, you can't *know*."

All these years later Eve carried that scene with her. It never seemed to be far from her mind, like the most profoundly painful memories often are. The grief cut too deeply. It wasn't a good day to trawl through the wreckage of her parents' marriage, either. She had this interview to face. She had to project the right image; poise and confidence, ability and potential. Not a young woman with a major trauma in her background. Traumatised people were high risk.

Eve tucked her briefcase under her arm, walking across another TCR logo worked into the grey marble floor in a giant mosaic. They certainly knew how to announce themselves.

The adrenalin flowing, she headed straight for the bank of lifts, resisting the childish urge to skid across the polished floor. Of course, she knew executive assistant with the company could mean almost anything from general dogsbody to someone who would be given real opportunities. It was a gamble, in a way, changing jobs, and God knows she was no gambler. But for once she had given in to her gut instincts.

Ever since she had left university with first-class honours in commerce and business administration she had been working for Pearce Musgrave. She'd had a fast rise in the three years she had been there but she had to accept, despite the praise that came her way, she might never be able to break through the glass ceiling. The hierarchy, the big decision makers at Pearce Musgrave, were all men. There was no woman at the top. A sprinkling in the second rank. Second rank didn't suit her. She was in it for the long haul. It was when she was passed over for promotion by a male colleague—to be fair, a smart guy, but Eve knew and so did everyone else his combined skills didn't stack up against hers—she decided to cast her net further. Ben had more years ahead of him at med school. Then his internship. Brilliant, sensitive Ben was in for the long haul, as well. Despite the two of them working their butts off the money just disappeared.

After the most devastating effects of "Cyclone Sally"—Eve's name for the divorce and her father's second wife—had worn off, their father had behaved "not all that badly" according to him. He had paid for their education right through high school until the demands of his second family, two new kids on the block, had altered the situation. Money became very tight and an ongoing problem.

Eve had worked her way through university, all her spare time spent serving behind the counter and doing the books for an old family friend, a respected jeweller, who had offered her the job out of kindness and who she had rewarded by turning his business around for him. For their mother there had been no inner resources to fall back on. Their mother had suffered. How she had suffered! Eve found out early how intense was a woman's grief when her man walked away from her.

From that day on Eve was the one who coped, her own battered emotions fuelled by anger and the determination her family would succeed on their own. Her number one priority had been to protect her mother and little brother.

Those who had known Eve as a little girl trying to take the collective pain on herself would say differently, but Eve knew she hadn't done a good job. Her mother, most tragic of all tragedies, had been killed in a road accident just before Eve's twentieth birthday.

''She just walked off the pavement right in front of me,'' the distraught motorist told the police.

Eve and Ben chose to believe it was an accident. They both cried about it even now. Their mother would never have left them. Not deliberately. It was just she had become *lost*. Unbelievably their father, the man her mother had loved and despised, had tried to rally around at the time, but Eve at flashpoint in her grief told him in no uncertain terms to stay away from the funeral. They were still being punished for his ''rotten cheating ways''.

No man would ever get the chance to cheat on her, she had vowed. She would rather go through her life alone than face what her mother had faced.

''I'm hard,'' Eve thought. ''A tough old nut of twenty-four.'' It was a lie she had carefully constructed. Her vulnerable core she concealed from the world.

Ben was the only chink in her armour. Her Achilles heel. Eve loved her brother with all her heart. Ben was the golden thread that ran through her life. Strangely, and she could never figure out why, she wanted marriage for Ben. She wanted him to find the right woman to love. Fatherhood, a good life. Brilliant as he was, Ben couldn't face life alone. Their father's early defection had left him sad and exposed though he, too, had learned to grow a protective shell. But the fear never left him. It just burrowed deep.

Waiting for the lift, Eve took time to glance around, smiling faintly at others who smiled back. A small crowd had gathered, business men and women chatting in groups. Some of the floors she knew were occupied by a prestigious firm of solicitors and TCR's own legal department. No sign of Sir David Forsythe, legendary mining magnate and chairman of the corporation. No sign of Drew Forsythe, the son and heir, lately voted chief executive officer by the board. Sir David was said to be inordinately proud of his son, so wonderfully successful in his own right.

Drew Forsythe, the womaniser. Although she had never met him—never moved in such high-flying circles—Eve was certain she knew all about him. He had divorced his beautiful young society wife after what, four years? Nothing sickened her more than men messing around. Eve had a girlfriend from a wealthy family who had met Drew Forsythe on several occasions and confided, "Dangerous is the word that comes to mind. Connery playing Bond. So smooth but with a kinda *edge*, know what I mean?" This with a playful dig in Eve's ribs. Lisa was always trying to take a rise out of her control freak of a friend.

But Eve's father had been handsome and charming, as well. Still was. She saw him from time to time when he tried to waylay her as she was coming from work. He was desperate to make it up to her. To Ben. But so far as they were concerned that part of their life was over. Their father's betrayal had shattered their world and caused the premature death of their loving mother. The barriers were drawn.

The descent of the lift intruded on the thoughts that

were always on the edge of her consciousness. Eve stood
back as it discharged its cargo before taking the next
consignment aboard. A middle-aged man in a pinstripe
suit indicated to her there was still room, but Eve shook
her head smilingly and turned away. She would wait for
the next and with any luck have it to herself.

Unguarded she moved closer as the other lift de-
scended, preparing to step in. No one else approached.
A couple who had entered the foyer was standing in
conversation with a man who was leaving. She heard a
snatch of their conversation. The financial crisis in Asia.
It was on everyone's lips and dominated the news. How
would it affect TCR? The word was they would be
largely insulated from the meltdown with their long-term
contracts.

So engrossed was she in her own speculations, Eve
was totally unprepared for the sight that now seared her
eyes. A sight so electrifying, for all its brevity, it flooded
her with impressions. What she caught in the stark fluo-
rescent lighting was a man and a woman, the sole oc-
cupants of the lift, springing apart from a passionate embrace. The woman with her head thrown back, tears
glittering on her long, shuttered eyelashes. Her dark
brown hair thick and lustrous was cut to shoulder length,
her skin a matt cream, her slim body immaculately
turned out in beautiful expensive clothes.

Lady Forsythe! Eve recognised her in a blinding flash.
Sir David Forsythe's second wife.

The man Eve would have known anywhere. Drew
Forsythe, his tall, lean body as smooth and springy as a
jungle cat. Drew Forsythe. The man who had everything.
Except honour. Eve felt a hot rush of disgust and intol-
erance.

There are some moments in life when the best thing

to do is turn and run. But she couldn't seem to move, immobilised by her own dark memories and a sick rage that had never left her. What a sordid little conspiracy right in the middle of a powerful corporation. Someone should have warned her. Or did no one yet sense a scandal?

Let it go, she urged herself, taking a few deep breaths. Disturbing as the sight was, it didn't warrant the strength of her reaction. After all, she wasn't personally involved.

Even when the door opened fully and the pair were in plain view, the woman still appeared dazed, standing stock-still as if to regain her bearings. And why not, with a man prepared to play such dangerous games?

Sir David, a widower for many years, had remarried little over a year ago. Eve remembered clearly all the press coverage. His bride was a partner in a highly successful public relations firm, mid-thirties no more, much the same age as Sir David's own son. Sir David, who had retained much of his remarkable good looks, had to be over sixty.

But money and power were the great aphrodisiacs, weren't they? They turned a lot of women on even if men were always the winners taking and discarding at will. Eve felt sick with contempt. If Drew Forsythe had begun some impossible, potentially *deadly* affair with his father's wife he shouldn't be allowed to get away with it.

Belatedly the woman came to her senses. She turned her head, large, drowning blue eyes, giving Eve the oddest little smile, gently vulnerable, but seemingly without guilt as though in being locked in her stepson's arms she had done no wrong. Obviously there were different rules for the mega rich.

"You'll be all right, then?" Drew Forsythe asked her,

those sexually inviting dark eyes totally focused on her lovely face.

"Don't worry, I'll be fine." She reached back with a quick intimate gesture and patted his cheek before stepping past Eve into the foyer. The air carried the subtle fragrance of her perfume. First. Van Cleef & Arpels. Eve recognised it with pain. Once her mother had worn it, revelling in her femininity.

"Until tonight then." Forsythe flashed the woman a smile of overwhelming attraction; a beam of sunshine that lit his dark features. Creases ran down his lean cheeks, fine white teeth contrasted with his dark tan. He was, Eve knew, a yachtsman of some note.

Only then did he notice Eve. "Going up?" He turned to her, voice very confident and vibrant, eyes narrowing as he began to take in her expression. Hell, that green gaze was like an icy crush of emeralds. He refused to believe a total stranger could look at him in such a way.

"Yes, thank you." Her voice was low-pitched, polite, but a touch brittle as though she was making quite an effort to appear casual.

He frowned, measuring her. Neat. No nonsense. Prim little blouse. Skirt to just above the knee. Tallish. Too thin. Luminous skin devoid of makeup. She looked like a novice on the loose from her convent, only there appeared to be forces seething behind the buttoned-up exterior. "What floor?" he asked, still looking at her.

"Five, thank you." Her dark blond head was primly secured at the nape. Good hair, he noticed. Did she have to scrape it back?

He pressed a couple of buttons and the doors closed, giving Eve an involuntary jolt. Settle down for God's sake, she admonished herself. For all his philandering he wasn't a sex maniac. Trying to collect herself, Eve stared up at the panel above the doors. What she was feeling within the narrow confines of the lift was most unwelcome. An instinctive thing, almost elemental. She had never felt so female in her life.

"Then you must be here for an interview?" he questioned her, wondering how this little nun with the chiselled bones could cut it in a tough professional world.

She nodded, still without looking at him. "Executive assistant. My appointment is for one-fifteen."

"Really?" He leaned back nonchalantly against the wall, a six footer plus, studying her profile. Her features had a refinement to them, even a decided elegance. "Then you can cast your mind over what you so obviously *thought* you saw—" he flicked back a cuff, glancing at his gold Rolex "—for a good eight minutes."

Heat swept her like a hot wind. The hide of him, an extremely experienced deceiver, to censure her. She was under no misapprehension as to what she had witnessed. She had the evidence of her own eyes. But be careful, an inner voice warned her. Be very very careful. This is Drew Forsythe. He could put paid to her chances.

She made herself glance towards him, her tone neutral. "I beg your pardon?"

"I expect you know exactly what I'm talking about," he answered in a clipped tone, much at variance with his previous warm, seductive tones. "In fact, I'd put money on it."

"*I* can't afford to bet." Though control was her watchword, the words leapt out.

"I rather suspect you're a paragon of all the virtues," he drawled, teak brown gaze sardonic. "Ah, here's your floor." It was funny in its way, but he couldn't seem to look away from her. Why? he wondered. She was hardly more than an overformal disapproving skinny kid. Then she turned her head! What a contradiction! Her mouth was heart-shaped with a full sensuous bottom lip. The mouth of a passionate woman. Now wasn't *that* the damnedest thing! She didn't look remotely like she'd been properly kissed in her life.

"You can't say good luck, Mr. Forsythe?" Eve asked, every part of her bridling at the flat-out intrigued and amused look in his eyes. Did he think every woman had to surrender to his sensual charisma? What a joke! Supremely sure of his own place in the firmament, he would accept without question she would know his name.

"I'm sure you'll rise very loftily above luck," he rejoined suavely.

"Damn!" Eve said softly as the lift doors closed behind her. "A thousand miserable damns." She tried to relax taut muscles, feeling stunned. Never in her life had she met anyone who had impacted so powerfully. Control it, she thought. Get a hold of yourself. Those dictates had gotten her through the years. But the *way* he had looked at her. She found herself flushing all over her body. So she wasn't gorgeous like the women he was used to. She had no glamorous image, no beautiful clothes. She was a working girl. Far from simple, her résumé would reveal as much, but with modest tastes to fit a modest budget. She always kept herself well groomed. Classic blouses, neat straight skirts, but there was no money for the slick power dressing some of her colleagues were able to afford.

When she reached Mr. Tom Whelan's office, his secretary, an exceptionally attractive young woman so chic Eve all of a sudden felt dreary, told her smilingly to take a seat. Mr. Whelan was a little behind schedule. Would she mind waiting?

No problem. Eve slid into a plush leather armchair. She had spent a lot of time researching the corporation, accessing the Internet, reading up on all the relevant data, articles, statistics, whatever. There wasn't much she didn't know about the legendary Sir David that was in the public domain. She had even soaked up all the information on the son who was currently abusing his trust. Such betrayal made her feel fierce, but she had to put a rein on it. She needed this job. She had to get ahead. Make a lot more money. Ease the burden on Ben. Between his part-time jobs and intensive study it was a wonder he wasn't heading for burnout. It did happen. Another brilliant young student in Ben's year had dropped out of the course. It took a lot to make a doctor. Even more to top your class. Eve was enormously proud of Ben, happy to admit he was her intellectual superior, and she was no slouch.

Quietly she leaned forward and picked up a copy of the *Financial Times,* glancing through it. She was starting to feel nervy, unable to put that disturbing confrontation behind her. Men as dangerous as Drew Forsythe had no part in her life. But how could she avoid seeing him if she got the job? His wife must have been heartbroken when he left her. She wasn't being hard on him. Her friend Lisa had told her it was definite Forsythe had left his wife. Not the other way round. Lisa's mother, a society hostess, was well up on all the gossip.

As she idly turned the pages, the door to Tom Whelan's office opened and a super-confident, preppy-looking young man emerged. Tom Whelan, a heavy-set man with a benign but businesslike expression, shook him by the hand, delivering the usual, "We'll be in touch."

The young man, still smiling securely, flicked a quick assessing glance over Eve, decided she wasn't a threat, then with a thank-you for the secretary continued on his way.

"Miss Copeland?" Tom Whelan threw out an arm, indicating Eve should come in to his office. They shook hands, Eve instantly recognising his reaction from his eyes. She had seen it before. Too young. Too inexperienced. Too fresh out of university. Inside the large office, as opulent as Eve expected, Whelan lost no time getting the pleasantries out of the way but he was barely into the interview before the phone on his desk rang.

He picked it up quickly. "I thought I told you, Ellie." A pause. "Oh, I see." A long, drawn out e—e—e. "That's interesting," he remarked to Eve as he hung up. "I know I could use the break, but I didn't think Drew, Mr. Forsythe, that is, would involve himself in proceedings. I usually handle all the preliminaries for him. It's your lucky day, Miss Copeland. Our CEO will conduct the rest of this interview. Don't let it make you nervous," he urged her, catching a curious rigidity in her expression. "Mr. Forsythe is used to putting people at their ease."

A moment more passed before Drew Forsythe arrived. They heard his voice before they saw him, exchanging a greeting with Whelan's secretary. The deeply etched smile was still in place as he entered and Tom Whelan sprang to his feet, stepping forward with a warm smile himself that so far as Eve could see was genuine.

"You're not in the habit of doing this sort of thing, chief?"

"And the young lady here is clearly unsettled." The brilliant gaze moved to Eve's dark blond head.

"No need to be," Whelan shot back, grinning like Forsythe was one hell of a guy.

"Take a break, Tom. Go get a coffee," Forsythe urged.

"Thanks, Drew. It'll be welcome." Whelan gave Eve a relaxed glance. "Best of luck, Miss Copeland."

After Whelan had gone, Drew Forsythe took a seat behind the broad executive desk and leaned back, hands locked behind his sleek dark head.

"I think you and I had better have a little talk, don't you?" He gave her a cryptic little smile, dark eyes glinting.

"I'd welcome that, Mr. Forsythe," Eve responded in an appropriate businesslike manner when she knew the question was not. "My résumé is on the desk there. Mr. Whelan had only just begun the interview."

"I'm not talking about résumés, Miss...Copeland, isn't it?"

"Yes. Eve Copeland." If his intent was to disarm her, she had no use for his charm.

"Ah, yes." He opened her file and had a quick glance through it. "Résumés are all very well," he said, shutting it, "but they don't tell everything one needs to know."

What was she supposed to say? Your secret is safe with me? Wasn't that his motivation?

"Actually what I wanted to discuss is what you *thought* you saw earlier at the lift."

Here it was, the moment to lose her head. But she resisted. "I'm not quite sure what you mean, Mr. Forsythe," she parried.

"Unhappily, Miss Copeland, you do. I caught your

expression. On a little circumstantial evidence you decided to play judge and jury and bring in a verdict.''

She held his dark gaze, confident this time her real
feelings didn't show in her eyes. ''Whatever I saw, Mr.
Forsythe, it was none of my business.''

''So tell me, as a professional courtesy, what did you
see, Miss Copeland? What provoked you into giving me
that icy self-righteous look.''

He appeared to be enjoying this. She had never seen
such…mockery, *mischief,* whatever in a man's eyes.
''Your imagination, Mr. Forsythe,'' she said, ''my mind
was preoccupied with the coming interview.''

He shrugged, toying with a gold pen on the desk.
''Tell me, did you recognise the lady I was with?''

''Of course.'' Eve nodded her head. ''Just about anyone in the city could identify her. Lady Forsythe.'' She
longed to add *your father's wife,* but that was way too
hazardous.

''So when you saw her in my arms your suspicious
mind immediately translated that into an affair?''

''Forgive me, I'm sure you would never do anything
so dangerous,'' Eve answered smoothly.

''Or immoral.'' His response, on the other hand, was
rapid-fire and curt. ''Lady Forsythe was confiding her
worries in me. She was in need of comfort and I was
there to provide it. That's all there was to it.''

What a lie! ''If you say so, Mr. Forsythe.'' Eve lowered her eyes. ''As I mentioned before, it's really none
of my business.''

''Then why did you react like someone had slapped
you in the face?'' he asked, sounding genuinely curious.

''I'm not sure what you mean,'' Eve evaded. ''I was
merely surprised.''

"I would hate to think you were given to gossip." He looked at her.

"I have no intention of mentioning the incident, Mr. Forsythe," Eve said, looking cool and unruffled. "I'm not given to casual gossip. Not about things that can hurt people."

"But you're relentless in your judgments." He kept his eyes on her, constantly weighing her up.

"I consider things very carefully first. Really, Mr. Forsythe, the whole thing scarcely warrants mention."

He laughed. "I would have thought so, too, only for what I saw in your eyes. I suppose if you manage to land this job you'd be following my every move," he commented dryly, reopening her file and studying it more fully. "Your résumé would seem to say you're special?"

"I've had a fast rise with Pearce Musgrave," she pointed out.

He looked down at the open page, frowning slightly. "So I see. Why do you want to leave?"

"Two things," she said crisply. "I need to earn more money and I prefer to work in a company that doesn't have a glass ceiling."

"I bet. I can see you're a career woman." The dark eyes swept her. "And do you plan to do something dramatic with more money?" he asked, deadpan.

"It would make life easier. I have a younger brother. He's a brilliant med student but he has a long way to go," Eve replied coolly.

He appeared to digest that, a slight frown between his black brows. "Can't your parents help out?" he asked finally. "Do you have to be his banker?"

"I'm afraid so." Eve gave a quite involuntary sigh. "My parents divorced when we were children. My mother was killed in a road accident a few years ago. Ben and I only have each other.''

He pulled her file closer to him, seized by a thrust of sympathy. "All I can say is he's very lucky to have you for a sister. I see you handled the refinancing for Hertford's.'' There was sharp reappraisal in his eyes.

"One of my success stories,'' Eve said with a quiet pride. "I also initiated the Newton Ransome merger. It's all there in the file.''

"So Pearce Musgrave did allow you to pull together some strategies?'' He lifted his dark head, looking at her dryly.

"I can't deny they treat me well. But I think it will take me a very long time indeed before I'm allowed to handle anything really *big*. I had a proposal for State Wide Airlines but it was taken out of my hands. As it turned out, all my good ideas were subsequently implemented.''

"Can you prove that?'' The dark timbered voice was clipped and businesslike.

"I believe I can,'' Eve said with certainty. "I have my original dated proposal. It was long before things began to happen.''

"So, a deep disappointment?'' Again that shrewd regard.

She shrugged. "They happen.''

He sat reading a while longer, occasionally looking up at her, then snapped the file shut as if it only contained bits of paper.

"So, you're looking for a position in the higher echelons, Miss Copeland?''

"I'm certainly working towards it. In time I hope to prove myself. I'm proud of the things I've done. I put in a lot of work on the Newton Ransome merger but I think the project I'm most proud of was turning a small business around when I was only seventeen.''

One black eyebrow shot up, rather humorously. "And how exactly did *that* happen?"

"You may know the business concerned. Small, surely, but doing very nicely. Stewart Strafford's, the jeweller?" Eve spoke quite seriously.

He shot her a look of momentary surprise. "Actually I know Charlie Strafford quite well. We often team up for a game of golf."

"Charles is Mr. Strafford's son, as I'm sure you know."

He nodded. "I've met Mr. Strafford. A very kind, gentle man. But Charlie's very bright. Are you trying to tell me *you* were responsible for getting Strafford's out of the red?"

Eve gave a nod of assent. "I am. Mr. Strafford would vouch for me. Charles *is* very bright but he wasn't all that focused on his father's small business. He was newly married with a promising career of his own. Mr. Strafford gave me a job through high school and university. Behind the counter, doing the books. He's an old family friend. He wanted to help out. It was a great pleasure to me to be able to reorganise his business affairs. I don't think it's a secret he was almost on the point of bankruptcy. When I started with Pearce Musgrave I hired him the right manager."

The teak brown eyes narrowed. "When I see Charlie I'll ask him."

"I hope you will," Eve replied simply.

"So you started young?

"I had to. I've always had a good business brain. That's why I chose commerce and business administration.'' She didn't add she had inherited her abilities from her father. She never acknowledged that small detail.

''So how else do you think you'd be a good addition to TCR?'' His voice was a touch mischievous but Eve continued in a serious vein.

''I'm not very old, twenty-four, but I've worked a long time. I handled our family budget. My mother was wonderful but—'' Eve paused, momentarily unable to go on. Her mother had let her father handle everything.

For a split second he saw the deeply hidden vulnerability in her beautiful large almond eyes. It sheened the irises like unshed tears.

''It says in my résumé I have plenty of drive,'' she continued in a firmer voice. ''I just want to be able to use it.''

''The position of Executive Assistant mightn't offer you all the chances you're after,'' he warned.

''I aim to use it as a stepping stone. I can deal with lots of problems. I have a proven track record pulling together budgets and strategies. I like Mr. Whelan. I know I can work well with him.''

He rocked back in the leather chair, his face breaking into that rakish engaging grin. ''Hang on. *I'm* the one looking for the executive assistant, not Tom. You won't be working with him at all.''

Eve bit back her dismay. ''That was never made clear.''

He shrugged elegant wide shoulders. ''Well, you said yourself the interview had only just begun.''

''You're absolutely right.'' Eve kept her face impassive.

''Does this make a difference?'' he asked with another quizzical lift of a brow.

She couldn't have picked a worse boss. "It's a surprise, that's all."

He noted the veiled eyes. "As it happens, the interviews are already concluded. Bright young men and women. I didn't specify gender," he added, with a dry look.

"I did see a young man come out as I was waiting."

"Time for a change, I suppose," he murmured as though speaking to himself. "You say you need the extra money, but that, Miss Copeland, is only part of it. There's a whole lot more you should know if it's decided you're the person I'm looking for. While we've been talking I've been looking over Tom's ratings. They're right here. I have to say on paper at least, you would seem to be the winning candidate. You've come from one of our top merchant banks with a résumé a sight better than anyone else's. My current assistant, Jamie Foster, is up for promotion on my recommendation. You'd have a hard act to follow. I can't spend a lot of time trawling the pool of talent. I need someone now."

"I'm sure." Eve responded to the flicker of impatience in his face. He had such an aura it threw off sparks.

"*Are* you?" he abruptly challenged. "You'd have to lose that straight-out-of-a-convent air."

Eve sat straighter. "I beg your pardon?"

Colour in her pale cheeks gave her a flash of real beauty. "Maybe it has more to do with your expression than your neat dressing?" he suggested.

"Surely there's no law against understated dressing." A trace of hauteur showed in her green eyes. She should have looked a little prig but she didn't.

He smiled lazily. Turning the attraction on and off,

Eve thought, trying to show no reaction. Those smiles were like beams of light.

"Of course not," he agreed smoothly. "But you do see a top executive assistant will be required to adopt a more high-profile image."

Eve felt a razor-sharp stab of resentment. What a terrible way to start a job. "I do appreciate that piece of information, Mr. Forsythe."

He burst out laughing at the tartness of her tone. "That's okay. I'm always breaking the rules. The furthest thing from my mind is to offend you, Miss Copeland. Your appearance is impeccable. I'm merely stating it will be necessary for the chosen candidate to dress *up* to the job. You surely know what I mean. I see what you've been making at Pearce Musgrave. Not a lot for a young woman with your qualifications and proven abilities. This position offers quite a bit more. It should cover power dressing. Isn't that what it's called?"

Eve studied the handsome face in front of her. No. Handsome didn't say it. No way! *Beyond* handsome. He had some extra dimension to him like an electrical field. And quite a reputation. In business. In bed. But never a whiff of scandal. Up until now. "So when do I start?" she asked, convinced he was toying with her. Damn it, she didn't need this. So she needed a career wardrobe? Even Lisa had had a word with her, but money was so tight. Damn him for noticing. But why wouldn't he? All the women in his life reeked of glamour. She felt a surge of dislike.

"Why not ASAP?" he responded, shocking her.

"You're serious?" What was all this about? Did he want her right under his eye to stop any rumours circulating?

"I'm always serious," he maintained, letting her read

into that anything she liked. "I assume you'll have to give Pearce Musgrave the usual notice?"

"As I said, they've been good to me." Eve swallowed hard on the knot in her throat. She was completely taken aback.

"They have a glass ceiling, that's all?" he commented with sharp humour.

"What I admire about TCR is, they don't."

"One more thing in our favour." He stood up, bringing the interview to an end. "Congratulations, Miss Copeland. I hope you're going to like it here." He came around the desk with the energy and grace of a trained athlete.

It was becoming increasingly difficult for Eve to play it cool. She had never been affected in this manner. "I'm sure I will, Mr. Forsythe. I promise you won't be disappointed with my capacity for hard work."

He gave her another one of those singular smiles. "A necessity, Miss Copeland, if you want to keep your job." He stood motionless for a moment, staring down at her. An odd, intriguing girl. Too self-contained with reserve wrapped around her like a cloak. Why exactly had he hired her? She was a bit of a whiz-kid from all accounts. Decidedly in her favour. But maybe it was the delicate shadows beneath those extraordinary green eyes? The fleeting moment when he had seen a hurt child? Whatever it was, he was stuck with her. In the short term at least. Conscious he was staring, he made a movement towards the door. "You can let my secretary, Sara Matheson, know when you can start."

"Thank you, I will." For the first time Eve smiled.

Would you look at that! He had a hard time to not say it aloud. "You might want to use that smile more often," he suggested.

"You think I need to?"

It was said with no hint of the coquettishness he invariably got from women.

"Given what it does for you, Miss Copeland, yes," he drawled. "If there's any likelihood of bringing the starting date forward, I'd appreciate it. My father has a project very dear to his heart I'd like to get to work on. I considered keeping my present assistant on for a bit longer. He knows all about the way I work, but he deserves this promotion."

Eve nodded, while inside of her there was a certain turmoil akin to standing at the very edge of a high cliff. "I'll discuss the matter with my boss and get back to you."

He stepped forward, held the door. "I'll bet he won't be too willing to let you go. But his loss is our gain." His expression was warm, friendly, masculine. With that little *edge*.

Eve was shocked she was actually feeling a little giddy. You fool, he's trying to charm you. Can't you see that?

He could almost see the battleshields going up. Who had hurt her? Very obviously he was a man. "Welcome on board, Miss Copeland," he said. "Or may I call you Eve?"

"Eve is fine, Mr. Forsythe." Actually, it was a problem. He had a wonderful sexy voice. She took his outstretched hand and nearly jerked it right back, perturbed by the flash of electricity on her naked skin. What was more humiliating was the fact he had gauged her reaction to the physical contact. She could see it in his brilliant mocking eyes, the jet black of the pupils lit by little sparkles. If only, if only she didn't need this job. But she did.

# CHAPTER TWO

EVE handed in her notice the same afternoon, on the one hand secretly thrilled to be taken on by TCR but left wondering if she had made the biggest mistake of her life. The money was great. It would make a difference to their lives even supposing she had to do something about herself like lifting her image. Lisa, the clothes horse, could help. But given her history, mightn't she find it difficult to work closely with a man who was so unrepentant about breaking all the rules? Drew Forsythe's private life had nothing to do with her, she inwardly argued, only she felt strongly a man's private and public life were connected. Then again she debated seesawing between one line of thought and the other, prominent men were always getting themselves into woman trouble.

Obviously most of them were of the opinion *one* woman was a woman short of the minimum. The wife and the mistress were necessary to ring the changes. She wondered if her father had had any little flutters over the past years or had he remained faithful to Cyclone Sally.

Sometimes it grieved her terribly she and Ben had close kin they didn't know; their stepbrother, Josh, about the same age Ben had been when their father had deserted them, and the little girl, Marilyn, now at school. Merrie she was called. Her father had told her that once as she tore away from him.

"Darling, Evie, please, where are you going? Won't you speak to me?"

28

"I'm never going to speak to you. Or your kids," she had yelled over her shoulder, her throat stiff and hurting from keeping back the flood of tears that, once started, she knew might never stop. Their father ought to leave her alone because it was she he always approached. He had made his decision years ago. The decision that had had their mother leaping in front of a car.

"Damn you, Dad," Eve gritted aloud. "And damn all you men."

Waiting for Ben to come home from his night-time shift at McDonald's—the brilliant surgeon in waiting, making up hamburgers—she reflected very deeply on what she had seen. She had more than a decided tendency to come down hard on men, no doubt a subconscious desire to keep blaming her father, but she had to master it for her own sake. She *needed* to master it. Her once sweet mother had by the end turned very bitter. Eve didn't *want* to believe the worse of Drew Forsythe.

Or did she? She thought about it for a long while. He was far too compelling, too self-assured, too full of that sharp humour that glittered in his eyes. He had incensed her about her wardrobe. Not so terrible, was it? Though most of her colleagues spent far more than she did on dressing. But then not a one of them was helping support a brother. Lisa had even told her she had to try for a sexier image. She could be a knockout if she tried. Words to that effect. The trouble was, she hadn't the slightest desire to be a knockout; to draw men's eyes. She wanted to be civilised and refined. She wanted to be as much in control of her life as she was of her outward appearance.

Sort it out, Eve thought. Get it clear in your mind. If she were honest she'd admit she had a secret fear of men like Drew Forsythe. Hell, she *was* honest, wasn't she? Staring out the window waiting for Ben to pull into the drive in his old Mazda, she managed to smile. She was happiest with a boss like the one she had. Jeffrey Ellison, fiftyish, balding, a good boss in his way, official, detached, given to the occasional act of kindness but essentially formal. The perfect banker. Drew Forsythe, for his part, was high octane. So much so it was a wonder there wasn't general disruption among all the female staff at TCR.

What had that look of Lady Forsythe's meant? She didn't look in the least arrogant, like some of the rich wives Eve had encountered. She looked…nice. Her eyes were lovely. Her smile had quivered with vulnerability. But God help us, couldn't a man like that compel a woman to fall in love with him. He in fact had been the one to draw away, assuming yet another persona. Devoted stepson. He'd been comforting her. Lady Forsythe had worries.

Didn't everyone? Eve thought bleakly. She would have accepted comfort as the reason except for Forsythe's blinding sexuality and the way Lady Forsythe's dark head had been thrown back. Those tears on her eyelashes. Heck, she was stuck with the sight like it had been burned into her retinas. Surely there had been *desire* there? She was horrified yet fascinated, as well. Equally she was amazed that she had landed the job. Even with her qualifications it didn't fully explain why he had picked her. Unless he was prompted by the nagging anxiety she might go about telling what she had seen?

When Ben arrived home he found his sister in the kitchen preparing a light supper for him.

"Hi!" He gave her his shining smile, picking up the cold glass of milk she had poured him and taking a long gulp. "That's good! What a scorcher! Worse tomorrow. So how did the interview go?"

Eve, busy gently stirring scrambled eggs, looked back at him and smiled. He was so incredibly dear to her he squeezed her heart. "A lot better than I thought. I got it."

"Brilliant!" They came together for a moment and slapped a high five. "I hope this leads to great things for you, Eve," Ben said earnestly. "You deserve it. You've worked so hard. For Mum. For me. One day I'm going to make it all up to you."

"All right. Venice. Two weeks at the Cipriani or is it the Danieli? Just past the Doge's Palace."

"You're on!" Ben said cheerfully. "I'd like that myself."

"My greatest pleasure will be seeing you graduate," she added. "Benjamin Kennet Copeland, M.D."

Eve put the plate of scrambled egg and two slices of smoked salmon in front of him, going to the toaster to take out the bread.

"This looks good." Ben forked into it hungrily. Astonishingly he wasn't one for hamburgers. At twenty he was tall, over six feet, but still retaining much of the attractive gangliness of adolescence. Like his sister, his eyes were green but more into hazel, his sun-streaked hair several shades lighter. Both of them had their father's fine regular features, the thin straight noses and the carved cheekbones, but both of them chose not to see it. Eve had their mother's full heart-shaped mouth. Ben had her gentle nature. Outwardly they could have been twins.

"So when do you start?" Ben asked, as pleased as punch she had landed the job.

"I put in my resignation as soon as I got back to the

office. Ellison wasn't happy, he thought I was there for keeps. Forever striving, not really getting anywhere. He even offered me more money if I stayed.''

''Why didn't they treat you better when you were there?'' Ben asked ironically. ''For a clever girl like you, Evie, TCR is the way to go. Isn't a woman a big shot there?''

''Vice-chairman. Chairperson, whatever.'' Eve pushed her heavy fall of hair away from her face. She never wore it like this to work. It altered her image too radically. Something about the hair and the mouth in combination. Lisa referred to it as her sexpot look. Eve knew she meant it kindly, even to flatter her, but somehow it hurt. A sexpot had ruined her family's life.

''So what's the problem?'' Ben prompted, recognising her ambivalence.

''You read me too well.'' Eve poured herself fresh coffee. She shouldn't be drinking it this late but she loved the aroma, the rich taste, these companionable moments with Ben. They were becoming too few.

''Drew Forsythe,'' Eve answered bluntly, beginning to butter a slice of toast for herself.

''Isn't he a brilliant kind of guy?'' Ben looked faintly aghast. ''That's all I read about him. No need for you to see too much of him surely. Isn't he CEO?''

Eve nodded. ''I wasn't aware at the time the position was *his* executive assistant.''

Ben stared at her thoughtfully. ''What a coup! Are you trying to tell me you don't think you can work with him? It sounds like an experience you shouldn't miss out on, to me. That Ellison took most of the credit for some of your projects, remember?''

''Well these guys do it all the time.'' Eve shrugged.

"Come on, Evie. What's worrying you? You should be on top of the world."

"I suppose I am thrilled in a way," Eve admitted. "I could only ever say this to you, Ben." Eve looked directly at her brother.

"Evie, when have you ever known me to pass things on?" Ben asked.

"It's absolutely confidential."

"Good God, girl, spit it out." Ben paused to savour the smoked salmon. Evie was always coming up with some little treat for him. He realised how much he loved her. How much he owed her. But even with him Evie played her cards close to her chest.

Eve began slowly, even now reliving it. "It was the strangest thing. As I was waiting for the lift doors to open I surprised Drew Forsythe in a pretty passionate clinch."

"Hey, hey, hey." Ben threw up his sensitive long-fingered hands. "What's so shocking about that? I've seen the guy in the flesh. I'd say most women would find him dynamite. The looks of a film star. A brilliant business brain. Heir to a fortune. Try to remember he's divorced. I hate to say this, Evie, but you have a real downer on us guys. Don't let what Dad did cut into your life."

"The woman he was with was Lady Forsythe," Eve told him baldly.

"What?" Ben looked uncertain whether to believe her. "The new stepmother?"

"I didn't want to talk about it. Even to you, Ben." Eve looked troubled.

"You could be wrong." He grabbed her hand and shook it for a moment.

Eve's mind flashed back to the scene. "I think not."

"Don't go all holy on us, Evie. Think again."

"I've been thinking about it right up until you arrived." Eve swallowed another mouthful of coffee.

Ben studied her face, seeing something of the old despair. "I can't believe that he would do anything so damned dangerous. Why, he and his old man are supposed to be exceptionally close. People say Sir David fairly dotes on him. The apple of his eye and so forth. It doesn't seem likely, Evie. Are you absolutely *sure?* I mean, what sort of a woman is she to be in something like that?"

"A susceptible one," Eve answered bleakly. "Perhaps captivated by his utter recklessness. Even now I can't believe it. She looked so damned decent."

"They were kissing, right?" Ben shoved his empty plate away and leaned his elbows on the table.

"Actually, they weren't. They were in the act of springing apart."

Ben groaned. "Then it's open to a different interpretation, sweetie. You're making a snap judgment."

"I'm not a fool, Ben. You know that," Eve said quietly.

"I'm sorry." Ben took her hand again and held it between his own. "But too much has been put on you, Evie. Too much responsibility. Too much pressure. I remember everything. The way Mum used to lean on you for God knows everything. The way she used to tell you never to allow yourself to trust a man."

Eve gave a little laugh to relieve the intensity. "I trust *you* with my life. You're a man, aren't you?"

"And a fascinating one to boot," Ben joked, "but you do see you might have been mistaken. Perhaps he was just hugging her. Can't a stepson do that?"

Eve responded flatly. "He's the sexiest damned man I've ever seen in my life.

"You can't hang him for that."

"He said he was *comforting* her."

"Then it could have been just that. Not a sexual goings-on. Don't ruin your chances, Eve, jumping to conclusions."

Eve didn't want to. Nevertheless her arms tightened unconsciously around herself. "I think you might have felt differently had you been there."

Ben considered. "We can't control people's private lives, Evie," he pointed out gently. "Did either of them act guilty?"

"Surprisingly, no." Eve shook her head. "She looked a little confused. He, of course, looked supremely self-assured. He's very experienced with women. A great ladies' man!"

Ben stood up, started pacing. "Evie, be honest. You don't know him at all."

"I know for a fact he divorced his wife. That's a start. It wasn't the other way around."

Ben laughed shortly. "Not everything Lisa tells you is true. People just love to gossip. Especially about the rich and famous. You can't condemn him for being divorced. Catch up with the statistics. His private life is just that. *Private*."

"Not even the President of the United States can get away with it," Eve reminded him wryly.

"So how did *you* act during the interview?" Ben asked, looking at his sister closely. "Your face can be a dead giveaway."

"How's that?" Eve looked up at him startled.

"You can look very high and mighty at times." Ben smiled. "It's something to see."

"So you think I'm overreacting?"

"I think you have a little bit of sensitive evidence but not enough to condemn the man," Ben said gently, giving her a quick hug. "Don't cut yourself off from this job, Evie. At this stage its far too early to throw away your chances. Only time will tell if you were right."

The makeover of her image seemed endless, though it took only a Saturday with the hyperactive Lisa—twice the winner of the "Fashion on the Field" competition—for guidance and support. Her hair first.

"This is wonderful hair," Lisa's hairdresser said as he let a thick bouncy curtain flow around Eve's face. "But we have to do something about the colour. You've let it darken, you naughty girl. Blondes have to look after their hair in a hot climate. We have to bring the sunshine back." He snapped his fingers at an assistant who ran with a colour chart. "You would have been very blond as a child?"

Eve nodded, glancing anxiously at the chart. Surely he wasn't thinking of going for an ultra hip platinum. That wasn't on. She didn't want her own self to disappear.

"Maybe hightlighting would do it?" Raymond considered, head on one side. "No, two shades lighter. I know exactly the effect I want."

While Raymond hurried off, not taking his commission lightly, Lisa of the dark snapping eyes and very short Raymond cut, gave Eve a comforting wink. "He'll look after you, Evie, so you can take the look of alarm off your face. Raymond is a genius." She leaned forward to catch a glimpse of herself in the mirror, well satisfied with what she saw. "After we're through here, we'll catch a cup of coffee as a booster, then on to makeup. I know you've got a beautiful skin but a light foundation will enhance it. We need eye shadow, mascara, blusher, a few lipsticks, the whole caboodle. "Heck, I've just thought of something." She broke off, rolling her eyes. "If you do *exactly* what I tell you, you might be able to land the gorgeous Drew. He's available."

Eve swivelled in her chair, staring directly at her friend. "Listen, kiddo, the answer is no, no, no. I'm prepared to swear it on a stack of bibles."

"You're not a bit of fun," Lisa said cheerfully. "If I was smart enough to get that job I'd make it my number one priority. I won't make the horrible mistake of opting for a career. I want to meet Mr. Right. But it has to be a man with a lot of clout."

"You'll meet him eventually." Eve smiled, thinking Lisa in the end would always follow her heart. "As for Drew Forsythe! I'm going to TCR to do a job."

"Even you mightn't be able to keep your mind on it." Lisa grinned. "Oh, this is fun." She gave Raymond, busy mixing up some concoction, a bright wave. "I can't wait to see the transformation."

Over an hour later the transformation was complete.

"Boy, the guy who said gentleman prefer blondes got it right," Lisa cried, startled. "Suddenly you're Michelle Pfeiffer."

"That sounds okay to me." Eve who had never spent so much time in a hairdresser's chair, fluffed out her crushed collar. As amazing as the results were, she had found the whole process an ordeal.

Lisa stood up, bent closer to the mirror, looking from Eve's reflection to her own. "You really like it?"

"It's very nice. I have to get used to it."

"But you look terrific. The truth is I'm jealous."

"I don't think so." Eve smiled. "You look great every single day of your life."

"Yeah, I do. But don't think it's not difficult. Running to the gym!" The petite Lisa shook her cropped dark head. "Why can't I be skinny like you?"

"I think it has something to do with your mother being a really great cook," Eve said, laughing.

"Which reminds me. You and Ben are invited around to a barbie tomorrow evening. Nothing special. Just family and a few friends. I might even get to talk to Ben. I guess if I levelled, I'm really in love with him but he's so *young!*"

"And he's got years of study to complete," Eve said with just a flicker of severity.

"I think you enjoy playing Mum," Lisa teased her, then flushed in embarrassment. "You know what I mean, Evie," she added quickly.

"Sure I do," Eve reassured her friend, not upset by her reference to Eve's having adopted the mothering role. "When he's Doctor Benjamin Copeland, M.D., you're in the running."

At the counter Eve produced her credit card, thanking Raymond again.

"Come to me in another fortnight," he said. "We have to keep the length just as it is. I enjoy transforming ladies. It makes me feel powerful."

"It must also make him *rich,*" Eve muttered as they walked out into the mall. "He must need to hire an armoured car to get the takings to the bank. That cost me an arm and a leg."

Lisa let out a bark of a laugh. "My dear, you've no

idea what it's done for you. The difference is remarkable.''

"The thing is I'm not really a Barbie doll,'' Eve said
a little warily as a complete stranger with several rings
in his right ear, walked past her and said, ''Hi!''

"Heck, no.'' Lisa nodded and took her friend's arm.
''You've got too much class.''

# CHAPTER THREE

Two weeks later Eve rode in the lift to her new office at TCR, trying quietly to gauge the effect her stylish new image was having on her fellow workers. The men were openly fascinated. The women's critical eyes told her she had passed the test. Weeks later and she still wasn't used to the shoulder-length swirl of dull gold hair around her face. She didn't think she would have kept to the style, only Ben told her she looked like a billion dollars and she would be mad to change it. The slick two-piece suit she was wearing, one of three she and Lisa had chosen, courtesy of a small personal bank loan, had a single-breasted long line jacket over a short narrow skirt with a white silk tank beneath. Her only jewellery was her mother's good earrings, pearl domes surrounded by a halo of gold. Her smart leather court shoes and bag matched her suit in a shadowy kind of charcoal, which Lisa assured her was a stylish alternative to black. So she was dressed at least to storm the corridors of power, the rest was up to herself.

Sara Matheson, Drew Forsythe's secretary, an elegant middle-aged lady with rather an elaborate makeup and cyclone-proof hairdo, was on hand to greet her and direct her to her corner office, waiting while she settled in.

"Add any little touches you like," Mrs. Matheson said, waving a manicured hand. "Photographs, personal mementos, flowers, that kind of thing. You'll spend so much time here you'll want to make it livable. The indoor plants are all supplied." Another wave towards the lush white flowering anthuriums. "They're changed regularly."

"This is wonderful. Thank you." Eve sat at her desk, delighted by the whole arrangement. The space, when formerly she had been so cramped, the quality of natural light, the view, the large sectional leather sofa that filled one corner of the room with a long, low coffee table before it. She hoped it was for the use of colleagues when they dropped in to contribute ideas. Or steal them.

"Mr. Forsythe has an early morning appointment but he's due in around ten." Sara Matheson busied herself rearranging trade magazines. "In the meantime I'll introduce you to the rest of the team. Jamie Foster will be dropping by to bring you up to date. You'll like him, Eve, and you'll need him for a while. The boss sets a cracking pace, so you'll have to keep up."

Introductions went off well except for one rather sharp-tongued young woman Eve suspected correctly had been after her job. Eve had encountered the type before. Ability not matching up to ambition. Ah, well...she couldn't win 'em all. She was sequestered in her office making an intelligent effort to acquaint herself with some of the files in the cabinet when Drew Forsythe walked down the carpeted corridor to tap on her door.

"Hello, Eve," he said.

She quietly laid down her pen, covering a sharp stab of emotion she refused to acknowledge.

"Mr. Forsythe." She came to her feet.

A minute stretched into two. Three. An eternity.

"Sit down. No need to stand up." He came in, shut the door behind him. "You seem to have made the adjustment to high profile," he observed, an intrigued, slightly amused look in his eyes.

She shrugged it off lightly as if the transformation was

of little consequence. "I was just trying to catch up on some files."

"Fine. Jamie will be able to give you a lot of help, but the project we need to work on is one I touched on lightly at your interview."

"You mean, the one dear to your father's heart?"

It was almost, not quite ironic and a poor choice of words because his teak brown gaze suddenly glinted. "*Exactly*. I can tell you aren't going to be dull. But I don't want to discuss it here. Come down to the conference room in about fifteen minutes. Jack Riordan, our environmentalist, will be sitting in with us. He'll brief you on environmental complications."

Over the next couple of hours Eve learned about Sir David's pet project, a science study research centre into rainforest plants combined with a small but world-class resort. The proposed offshore resort, to be located on the coast between the North Queensland rainforest and the Great Barrier Reef Islands, would fund the whole operation and make it commercially viable to the very tough businessmen on the TCR board.

"And what do the rings on this map stand for?" Eve asked, turning it more towards her.

"The large green one is the land we've acquired," Drew Forsythe explained. "The two smaller ones represent acquisition targets. The area outlined in red belongs to a local grazier. Until now he's held out, but we have reason to believe he'll sell if we up our price. The area ringed in blue belongs to Elizabeth Garratt. She used to have quite a career as a stage actress. Pretty reclusive now. She's refused to sell. To win her over is crucial. This is a science centre but it needs the resort to finance it. Once feared toxins are now at the cutting edge of medical research and many of the toxins under investigation come from the trees and plants of our rainforest. Our policy is to conform strictly to the environmental ethic.''

"Have you approached Mrs. Garratt with that?'' Eve asked.

He glanced down at her with a wry smile, pleased with her quickness and intelligence. "Jack tried, but so far no one has been able to get to her. As I say, she keeps very much to herself since her husband died.''

"That's sad,'' Eve murmured spontaneously.'' She must be assured no deterioration of the rainforest will take place.'' Eve checked the map. "There are in-built safeguards to point out. It's a very sensitive region. I can understand her concerns about a resort but she's not really aware of our proposal until we talk to her. The research station is potentially of great benefit to mankind. Our tropical rainforest is the most luxuriant diverse and complex plant community on earth. We've only begun to touch on the medical wonders of the plant life.''

"You'll have to speak to my father.'' Drew Forsythe smiled at her enthusiasm. "I'll introduce you when he gets back from Indonesia. Actually—'' His expression became thoughtful. "You might be just the one to get through to Elizabeth Garratt.''

"It's certainly an idea.'' Now Jack Riordan eyed Eve, his rather worn, clever face creased up with speculation. "She might take more kindly to an intelligent young woman who looks so utterly trustworthy.''

"I can't tell her anything that's not true.'' Eve's expression was light but serious.

"Hardly.'' Drew Forsythe raised his black brows. "We operate up front. But you can't tell everyone *everything,* Eve.''

"I appreciate that," Eve said quietly.

"Anyway, you have my absolute assurance we're not into abusing anyone's trust. Think you could do it?" Drew queried.

"Speak to Mrs. Garratt?"

"In that nice calm style of yours." His dark eyes both approved and mocked.

"Certainly.

Jack grinned across the broad mahogany table. "Sounds like you've got a top negotiator here."

"That's one of the reasons she'll get to talk to the lady. TCR is fully conscious we have to walk a very fine line, Eve. What we are planning with our resort is a very *minimum* of interference with the natural environment. Forests once lost can never be regained, but most of the abuses have been stopped. We've had to change direction with mineral exploration development ourselves. What we're planning is a tourist retreat in one of the last remaining great wilderness areas in the world. The research centre, funded from this, we believe could have enormous potential for medical science. This has been my father's dream and I'm going to see it realised."

"It wasn't my intention to sound negative." Eve looked up at him, feeling his determination and power.

"Listen, I expect you to speak your mind. I also expect you to hear what I say. Jack, here, will have his department deliver a series of mini reports to you, which you'll have to study in detail. It will need a whole lot of work to pull the thing together. Your job, Eve, will be in the area of co-ordination. Mine will be to sell the concept to the board. Not all of them are in favour of the science study center in case it drains off too much money. The resort has to be a winner. You may get a chance to use your charm on Mrs. Garratt early next month. That's when Jack and I will be heading north. You might as well come along for the ride.''

The weeks flew. Eve set her alarm for half an hour earlier, rising at six fixing breakfast for herself and Ben, dashing under the shower for a few minutes, dressing herself swiftly in her new clothes. She no longer felt strange with her new image. She didn't have the time. Stunningly sexual as Drew Forsythe was, he didn't look at her with anything but a friendly and at times sharply demanding eye. Here was a boss who kept his team on the boil. When he asked for something, he expected it to be delivered. In detail.

Eve worked harder than she ever had in her life, but the excitement was always there. The challenge. It was exhilarating to be constantly tested. As a boss, Drew Forsythe gave her her best ever opportunity to use her talents. In fact some of his scintillating vitality was spinning off on her. She was finding out things all the time, learning from Jamie Foster, who turned out to be a very agreeable young man with a kind of sweetness to him that reminded her of Ben. She was vaguely aware he was attracted to her, but her head was so full of doing her job nothing much outside of delivering the goods to her boss seemed to click. In a way she treated Jamie very much as she treated Ben, with a gentle charm and a subtle touch of Big Sister.

''It's about time we had a meal together, isn't it?'' Jamie suggested one evening, closing his eyes and stretching his long arms. It had gone on seven and they still hadn't left the office.

''Just give me a couple more minutes,'' Eve implored, busy working out costing on an interim report. Overtime was a regular part of the job but she could never complain about the pay. TCR took care of its own. And they took care of Ben. For the first time since their father had left them, the financial pressures were beginning to ease.

"So, still sitting here, Jamie?" Drew Forsythe came out of his office further down the corridor stopping as he often did for a casual chat. He sat on the edge of Eve's desk so damned handsome and vibrant it was hard for Eve to drag her eyes away. He had taken off his jacket, flipped up the cuffs of his pale blue shirt, loosened his dark red small-patterned tie. Fine curls of dark hair showed high on his chest. Fine dark hair on his arms. His gold watch glinted on his bronze wrist. He was intensely, *intensely* masculine with a potency that made the attractive Jamie with his fair good looks appear boyish and immature.

Jamie unaware of Eve's thoughts laughed. "I'm trying to get Eve to join me in a meal. But she won't come until she finishes off everything for you."

"Here, what are you working on?" Drew reached out a hand, his fingers touching Eve's as she passed it to him, sending out the now predictable little shock. She didn't know *what* it was but it felt exactly like an electrical current.

He looked down, read for a moment. "This is good, Evie. You're an ideas woman."

When had he started calling her Evie? It sounded so lazy and seductive, she swallowed. How the hell did anyone get to be like that?

She glanced up, a trace of hostility mixed up with the gratification in her green eyes. "I really wanted to finish it before you saw it."

"No, this is fine." He watched her for a moment. He held the sheafed pages of Eve's report, seeing the flicker of reaction but remaining tolerant. Even curious. "There's probably enough here already."

"She's a very willing worker." Jamie spoke out in friendship and admiration.

"You've been an enormous help." Eve wrenched her gaze from Drew Forsythe to tell him.

"You've checked all these figures," Drew interrupted them, his voice crisp and businesslike.

"Down to the last cent," Eve confirmed. "I'm sure the costing can be tightened."

She lay down her pen and, like Jamie, stretched like a cat.

Dark eyes travelled all over her for a few seconds, placing tremendous tension on Eve. What she desperately needed of him was to play it straight, the brilliant businessman and boss, not the man who could seduce a woman with a single look.

"You've been cooped up too long," he said gently, feeling a kind of fear in her. Of *what?* He wanted to know.

He could see the outline of her small high breasts beneath her sleeveless crossover silk vest. It was a sherry colour that went beautifully with the cream of her skin and the dull gold of her hair. The long delicate bones seemed sharper, more fragile. It crossed his mind he'd been working her too hard. And it was getting late.

"Why don't I take you both out?" he suggested casually, shifting his gaze to Jamie. "We can go to Leo's."

"I say, that's very decent of you, Drew." Jamie grinned with pleasure.

"You don't have to." Eve had caught the indefinable but somehow gentling look in his eyes. Was he sorry for her? If so, she had to be more careful.

"Why not? I need to snatch a bite to eat myself." He began to walk back to his office to collect his jacket.

The phone on Eve's desk suddenly rang and she picked it up, listening for a moment, then holding her hand over the receiver. "It's your mother. I'm afraid she's furious with you."

"Hell, hell, she should be!" Jamie sat forward abruptly, groaning and holding his head. "I was supposed to call her. Maggie must have arrived. That's my illustrious godmother, and Mum's best friend." He took the phone from Eve, talking briefly with his mother.

Jamie waited for Drew to return to explain why he couldn't join them. "I'm really sorry. But Maggie…"

"I don't think you're averse to the idea of being her heir," Drew laughed.

"For God's sake, Drew, who else could she leave it to?" Jamie joked. "I'll have to fly. Mum has been waiting dinner."

They watched him go, taking the elevator to the underground car park.

"I really don't want to take up your time." Eve turned to Drew Forsythe, a kind of panic riding high in her chest. The workplace was one scene. A trendy restaurant was another.

He looked down into her very clear green eyes, so limpid despite all her secrets and what would seem to be hang-ups. "Aren't you hungry, then?" he pressed her, reading the message clearly.

"Of course I am. Starved."

"And you're starting to look it." His gaze flickered over her delicate breasts and shoulders. "I expect my team to work hard but it seems to me you can't have much time to relax."

Eve turned away, desperate for a *distancing*, shouldering into her short-sleeved linen jacket. "Perhaps I don't need too much relaxation."

"Sufficient irons out the kinks," he commented dryly. "Come on, Eve. This isn't a difficult assignment. We're simply having a quiet meal."

During the daytime the city was vibrant with tropical beauty born of cloudless cobalt skies, brilliant sunshine and the splendid flowering of all the ornamental trees, shrubs and soaring palms that adorned the many parks and the lush Botanical Gardens near the city centre.

At night under an indigo sky pierced with a trillion stars, it assumed a soft seductive air, the breeze warm and langorous, the broad deep river that wound through the city heart opalescent with the dazzle of the glittering towers and buildings, the floodlit arches and tiaras of the bridges that spanned the river's impressive width.

Blessed with the perfect climate for outdoor living, the traffic-free City Mall was alive with people crowding into the shops and cinemas, dining al fresco, listening to the organised entertainment or the surprising depth of talent from the city's buskers, with young lovers holding hands sitting on the garden benches and rotunda, or around the beautiful fountain crowned by life-size statues of a young mother keeping watch over her two small sons as they sported in the pool. Others stood staring into the scintillating windows of the jewellery stores with their massed trays of engagement rings, diamonds, rubies, emeralds, sapphires, dreaming of a time one would grace a beloved hand. Many more were walking the short distance to the casino housed in the magnificent old treasury building, or continuing on to the Performing Arts Centre for a concert. There were a number of international artists in town. The Russian virtuoso pianist, Demidenko, Eve particularly wanted to see.

As Drew joined the smooth flow of traffic onto the Riverside Expressway, Eve looked out the window at the City Cats busy ferrying passengers to and fro across the river. *The Kookaburra Queen,* the luxurious paddle-wheel cruise boat was all asparkle wending its way upstream, the music on board drifting to the banks.

Brisbane had a unique relationship with its beautiful river, Eve reflected, friendly for the most part but together with its network of major tributaries and many creeks, a mighty force in times of severe flood. Eve herself had been born in the year of the last great flood of 1974 triggered by the infamous cyclone Tracy that levelled the city of Darwin in the Northern Territory on Christmas Day. Everyone in the city loved their river as she did, but they all had a healthy respect for its power especially when a cyclone threatened. Tonight it was at its most beautiful and benign.

They found parking opposite Leo's. It was one of those small exclusive riverside restaurants Eve had never visited. I lead such a spartan private life, she realised. The maître d' greeted them with delight, escorting them to a table for two by the window.

"Would you like a drink to unwind?" Drew asked.

"Perhaps. Just one. A dry white."

"You can handle a Riesling?"

She nodded. "No problem."

"You have your car?"

"Ordinarily I do, but not at the moment." She let her light laugh run, minimising her lack. "It held on as long as it could but the motor gave out."

"You mean you *don't* have a car?" He cocked a brow. "Aren't I paying you enough?"

"No more than I'm worth." Her green eyes sparkled.

"Ah. You're asking for a raise?"

She answered without hesitation, conscious of a rising excitement. "I'm sure I'll get one when I'm worth it."

He stared at her, in the soft lighting his eyes as dark as night. "Actually I'll get onto it tomorrow. You'll need a work car."

Something flared inside her. A wariness, a kind of perverse anger. "I wonder if you made the same offer to Jamie?"

"What gets into you, Evie?" He snapped the words out. "Jamie comes from a very wealthy background. Didn't you know?"

"I didn't, actually," she admitted, dipping her blond head.

"Really? You've spent so much time together. I thought he might have revealed it in passing."

"He might have, but I missed it. Jamie doesn't flaunt that sort of information."

"You get on well together?"

Eve smiled and sank back in her chair. "He reminds me of Ben in a way. They're both extremely intelligent. Both have a sweetness of nature."

"And Ben is the most important person in your life?" His dark eyes were full of interest.

"We need one another desperately," Eve freely admitted, toying with an empty wineglass.

"But you'll both marry in time."

"Are you criticising?"

"No. I'm making a perfectly reasonable remark."

"And you want an answer?" She glanced at his dynamic face. "I'm hoping Ben will, yes. When he's completed his studies."

"And not before then?" he answered with a trace of mockery.

"I hope not." Eve's fine-boned face was serious. "Ben has always wanted to be a doctor. Nothing must stand in his way."

"You mean, he can't fall in love until *you* say?"

"I want the best for him."

"I realise that, Eve." His vibrant voice deepened. "So what about you? I know you're less than impressed with your own beauty, but surely you've had your share of boyfriends?"

"Of course," she said smoothly when it wasn't strictly true. "I'm not much good at relationships, I'm afraid. I prefer not to get involved."

"Why *is* that, Evie?"

Some note in his voice made her raise her eyes. "What makes you so interested?"

He shrugged, held her gaze. "There's so much *more* to you than I can see. I have a naturally investigative nature."

"But you're my boss. We're not friends."

"No, we're not," he said as if he cared, causing her to crush her fingernails into her palm. Seduction could happen to anyone. She didn't want it to happen to her.

"I think you set your mind against me right from the beginning."

"That's not true." Even so, her hand shook.

He gave her the shadow of an ironic smile. "Now that it's no secret, I'll tell you. Lady Forsythe had suffered a miscarriage at that time. She was pretty cut up about it. Not herself for quite a while. She felt she had let my father down. He was thrilled at the news, delighted to father another child at his age. But it wasn't to be."

Eve lifted her head and looked at him in open apology. "I'm sorry, I didn't know."

"But you fell into the trap."

She flushed, eyes shimmering. "Of jumping to conclusions?"

"It might have been easier for you. *And me* if we'd met after the interview."

"Possibly." She was aware a waiter was advancing. "Is there something about my manner you don't like?"

"There's something about your manner I can't analyse," he corrected, his gaze unwavering.

Eve sat quietly for a few moments while he ordered a bottle of wine. "I suppose we all have our secret places," she murmured eventually, picking up the conversation. "Places we don't let anyone else into. Don't you?"

"That's insider stuff, Evie."

The way he used her name raised goose bumps on her skin. "If this is a *private* conversation, you've asked *me* a lot of questions. What about you?"

"What do you want to know?" He smiled at her through narrowed eyes.

"I think it'd be wise not to put it into words."

"Come on," he challenged her.

"No. I can't forget you're my *boss*."

"And you're proving yourself too damned fast. In fact, you're rapidly becoming invaluable," he conceded.

"As good as Jamie?" It was said with a faint taunt. "I recall you told me he'd be a hard act to follow?"

He let his eyes linger on her, coolly beautiful, a touch away from outright challenging. "Somehow or other you combine *all* Jamie's abilities with a few more of your own. You're very good, Evie, only you're a little too intense."

"Shouldn't that make me more interesting? Anyway, I can't help my nature."

"I don't think that's the answer." He was watching

her so closely she might have been some exotic creature he wished to study. "Who do you resemble?" he asked. "Mother? Father? Where did you get your eyes, that patrician nose and your contradictory mouth, those long delicate bones?"

She inhaled sharply despite herself. "Who do *you* resemble, then?"

"Surely my father," he suggested. "Most people think so."

She allowed herself to stare back at him. "Certainly, the height and the colouring, but you have a look about you of someone entirely different."

"Now that is perceptive." He laughed. "My mother used to say I had her father's style. He was a very glamorous figure within the family. Unfortunately he was killed many years ago flying his own plane over the New Guinea jungle."

"What was he doing there?" Eve asked.

"He owned a couple of coffee plantations. He was always flying around New Guinea and South East Asia. My grandmother used to say he was wedded to that plane."

"Like you're wedded to your yacht?" She recalled all his press coverage.

"It's my father's yacht, really." He smiled. "But I've always enjoyed sailing since I was a boy."

The waiter returned with their wine, moments later. An excellent choice. Eve felt its freshness on her palate. Their order was taken, the magnificent summer seafood for both.

"This is nice." Eve let her eyes travel around their end of the room, taking in all the details.

"One of my favourite places to eat." As Eve stared

off, he allowed himself to study her. "You've never been here before?"

"I rarely dine out. Can't afford it."

"What about those boyfriends?" Whether she liked it or not she had a devastating effect on men. He had seen it.

"I think they'd be shocked by the prices." She smiled.

"What does Ben do in his spare time?"

"Sleep," she said wryly. "He hasn't much spare time. It's a long haul getting to be a doctor. Years."

"And you've been finding it tough since you've been on your own?"

She was silent for a while. "We get by."

"I'd like to meet Ben." He tried to draw her back again.

"Why?"

Something about those cool green eyes wrenched his heart. "I'm not just being polite, Eve."

"I didn't suppose you were. I think it has to do more with your investigative nature."

"Maybe." He smiled.

Easy, so easy, to lose herself in its magic. Careful, Eve told herself, breathing common sense and caution into her soul. This man exerted the strongest of attractions. The expert on women. Expertly playing the game of fascination. Hadn't she sensed in some small part of her, from that very first moment, he would come into her life.

Under the effects of two glasses of fine wine she began to tell him a little more about herself while he listened as though he was truly interested. She could have been the most captivating woman in the world instead of Eve Copeland. Wasn't that part of his magnetic charm? It's a game with him. But I don't play games, she thought. For this short time they weren't boss and employee. They were most definitely a man and a woman learning more about each other.

They were finishing coffee when a young woman stopped by their table, ultra-slim, ultra-fashionable, separating herself from her group who all smiled, waved at Drew, looked at Eve with open curiosity, before moving on.

"Well. How nice." The woman spoke directly to Drew. "You haven't been answering my phone calls."

For a minute Eve thought he was going to totally ignore her. "Why do you make them?" he finally asked.

"You *were* my husband." She shot another glance at Eve. "Cradle snatching, are we?"

"Don't expect me to rise to that."

"At least you can introduce me," she said quickly, light blue eyes drilling holes in Eve.

"I could. But I'm not going to," he replied. "Was it a nice birthday party?"

The ex-Mrs. Forsythe looked brighter, as if excitement had shot through her. "So you do remember?"

"Lots of them," he said, his voice harsh. "You must go, Carol. You're keeping everyone waiting."

Carol Forsythe shook her head, still staring at Eve. "Are you lovers? You *are*." She seemed amused by Eve's quick flush. "I know he's idyllic, darling, *extraordinary* but he's quite terrifyingly without a heart."

"You've had too much to drink, Carol." Drew Forsythe sounded very bored.

"All I've ever done is love you," she said, her pale blue eyes scouring his face for some kind of reaction.

He stood up, looming tough and suave. "You have such ability to deceive yourself." His voice had a faint rasp. "I'd go if I were you before you turn us both into a joke."

That brought forth another response. The woman bent low over their table, murmuring directly to Eve, "You have no idea what you're getting yourself into."

"Forgive me, but you have no idea what you're *saying*," Eve answered mildly. "I'm only an employee."

"You shouldn't have told her even that," Drew said later, grasping Eve's arm and guiding her across the car park.

"I felt sorry for her. Obviously she was terribly jealous."

"Carol hates not to be the centre of attention," he said flatly.

"Whatever happened?"

"Both of us made a rotten choice."

"I'm sorry."

"So be damned careful where you give your heart," he advised her.

"Careful is my middle name."

He suddenly laughed, turning to her as she stood in the bright light from the TCR building. "With a mouth like that?"

Emotions are more powerful than the strongest defenses. Eve felt her whole body quiver. She might have been a stringed instrument and he the virtuoso. It was a warning sign, a forceful reminder that that had been no nice quiet dinner. There was nothing remotely nice and quiet about Drew Forsythe. He was dynamite and it shook her badly she was far from immune.

"Look, you're upset," she said quickly, anxious now to make her escape. "There's a cab rank over there."

He was all coiled energy. "You know damn well I'm driving you home." A distinct change had come over him since the confrontation with his ex-wife. He always appeared so supremely self-confident, so much in charge of himself. Eve was surprised to find him emotionally vulnerable. Perhaps he still loved her? Perhaps as much as he wanted to he couldn't suppress that love? Human relationships were so fragile. One good reason why she shied clear of them.

"Where to?" he asked as his Jaguar slid smoothly into the traffic. The streets were full of people off to restaurants, theatres, pubs, the movies.

She inhaled nervously, loving the rich leather tang of the car, the comfort, but dogged by a sense of unreality. What was she doing here in this cool, confined space with her boss? It was like being caught in a powerful vice. In the semi-darkness his handsome face had a brooding look that, if possible, made him even more attractive. "I'm absolutely certain I'm taking you out of your way."

"That doesn't matter in the least, Eve. The suburb will be enough," he prompted, giving her a sideways glance.

"I'm sorry." Eve gave him the address of her quiet street on the south side of the city. Everyone knew the Forsythe Anglo-Indian colonial mansion set high on a jacaranda-covered hill overlooking the river. The family home from the 1890's it was Sir David and Lady Forsythe's residence. Drew Forsythe's former home was almost as well known, a striking modernist villa set in the rolling western hills. Eve had read somewhere the villa had been part of his ex-wife's divorce settlement. Drew Forsythe himself had the penthouse in arguably the finest apartment block in the city.

All of which was a far cry from the six-unit block Eve and Ben rented. The family home had to go years ago for a much smaller retreat. After their mother died they had sold that, unable to cope with all their painful memories.

"I'm sorry you had to witness that," he said, breaking a rather fraught silence.

Eve shrugged. "These things happen."

"Carol's behaviour alters when she's had too much to drink."

Eve, too, had lost some of her light control. "She still loves you. She's feeling abandoned. Ripped from her moorings."

"One of her fantasies," he replied bluntly.

"I doubt that very much." *Me,* so sensitised to loss.

"Eve, you don't know."

It was almost, for *him,* a deep sigh.

"Forgive me. I'm overstepping the mark," Eve apologised.

"And maybe giving away quite a lot. I'm not such a fool I don't know you consider me both wicked and dangerous." There was an amused edge to his voice.

"I do not," she burst out.

"Yes. Oh, yes, you do. There's no point in denying it. I suppose an explanation lies in your past."

"Heavens, you're not going to try to psychoanalyse me?" She forced herself to reply lightly.

"You're very unusual. I'm interested in you, I admit."

"As a case study?"

"As a colleague and a friend. We have to become friends, Eve, if we're going to work closely together. Anyway I'd like to apologise on Carol's behalf. She always did see any good-looking woman as competition. It's just the way she is."

"There's no chance you may have given her good

reason?'' It came out so quickly she couldn't pull the words back.

''A real little man hater, aren't you?'' His handsome mouth twisted.

''No.'' Eve's response was quick and firm. ''I just don't think men regard things like fidelity as all-important.''

''Is that why you're frightened to fall in love?'' He glanced very briefly at her.

''I object to that.''

''Really?'' He laughed. ''That's rich, when you've just written me off as a womaniser.''

Belatedly, Eve tried to retrieve the situation. ''As a matter of fact I admire you greatly. I couldn't ask for a more inspiring boss. I thoroughly enjoy working for you. It's a challenge. I don't think we should continue this discussion, my tongue is running away with me.''

''I should ply you with wine more often,'' he replied dryly. ''Now perhaps you can direct me from now on. I'm lost once we get past this bridge.''

They arrived outside Eve's apartment block at the same time Ben swung into the driveway.

Ben saw Eve and the well-known Drew Forsythe standing beside a beautiful late-model Jaguar and swung towards them in his friendly fashion.

''Hi!''

''It's my brother, Ben,'' Eve said as Ben approached.

''Good. I wanted to meet him.''

Eve made the introductions and the two shook hands. ''It's good of you to drop Evie home,'' Ben said. ''I don't suppose you heard the story of her Laser?''

''As a matter of fact I did.'' Drew Forsythe flashed

his heart-stopping white smile. "I think we can run to a work car, especially when overtime is part of the job."

"Say that would be great!" Ben said, his tone amazed. "Look, can I get a job there?"

"Eve tells me you're studying medicine?"

"In between stints at McDonald's," Ben laughed. "I've got a few years to go yet, but I've wanted to be a doctor ever since I can remember."

"With Eve by your side I know you're going to make it. Well, time to go." Drew lifted a hand, moved back to the driver's side of the Jaguar. "Nice to meet you, Ben. Early start tomorrow, Eve."

"I won't be late."

"Gosh, isn't he bloody *something,*" Ben marvelled after Drew had driven off. "I mean, I've seen him, but the whole package!"

"Pretty impressive," Eve agreed dryly.

"I wonder what he made of our humble abode?" Ben turned to look back at the apartment block.

"He's not a snob. I've seen him being utterly charming to the cleaning ladies."

"Now that's class." Ben dropped his hand on his sister's shoulder, turning her towards their ground-floor unit. "Did I hear him right, offering a car?"

"Probably he's thrilled to have me for an assistant," Eve joked. "*Executive assistant.* Actually, we had dinner."

"You *what?*" Ben stared down into his sister's face. "My girl, you'd better guard your virtue with your life."

"Now why do you say *that?*" Eve walked ahead, taking out her door keys and inserting the master key into the lock. "You were the one who defended him, remember?"

"I was only having a bit of fun, Eve. Lighten up. All

I meant is, he's one hell of a guy. So you got to go to dinner. What else?''

Eve put her handbag down on the hall table close to the front door. ''I met his ex-wife.''

''That was pretty cool.'' Ben locked the door behind them. ''You mean, they're still friends?''

''On the contrary she's a beautiful tortured soul. Wait until I get changed and I'll tell you the rest.''

''Thanks, but I can't wait,'' Ben called after her. ''You mean, there was drama?''

Eve turned back, reliving the moment. ''Actually she inferred Drew and I were lovers.''

''Gawd!'' Ben moved to a sofa and flopped into it. ''I'd like to have been there.''

''Talk about a shock.'' Eve divested herself of her jacket and sat down beside him.

''I'd better brace myself,'' Ben said wryly. ''There's more?''

Eve bit her cushiony underlip. ''He was upset after. A little on the dark side. She didn't have dinner with us. Jamie was supposed to come, but a phone call from his mother sent him packing. The ex-Mrs. Forsythe was dining with friends. Her birthday, from what I can gather. She stopped at our table on the way out.''

''What an enterprising thing to do,'' Ben remarked. ''Seems like she upset you, too.''

''She did.'' Eve nodded her head. ''I felt sorry for her. She still loves him.''

''Of course she does.'' Ben gave a long sigh. ''Hell, she'll probably love him until the day she dies, but obviously it didn't work out.''

''It couldn't have been her fault,'' Eve said grimly.

''There speaks the little feminist. Matter of fact, a guy I know, when I told him you landed the job at TCR, told me she's a real bitch. All *her* pals are in. All the rest of us are out of it. Kevin Carson is her dad. You know, Carson Constructions. Word is he's not a terribly nice guy.''

''But filthy rich.''

''Yes, isn't it awful, but not top drawer like your Drew. Though as it turns out, he's not so different to the rest of us. He makes *mistakes*.''

# CHAPTER FOUR

To Eve moving dreamlike in Drew's and the forest ranger's wake, it was like being alive at the dawn of creation. The noon sun was blazing on the rainforest canopy but one hundred and fifty feet below on the forest floor it was like a shadowy green ocean filled with the most beautiful soft sea grasses, trillions of exquisite little ferns that sprouted from everywhere forming a delicate almost translucent carpet.

Dressed in yellow jeans with a sleeveless white top, lightweight sneakers on her feet, Eve kept to the narrow path, doing her level best to obey their guide's instructions not to touch anything. Easier said than done when one had the irresistible urge to stroke a particular fantastic leaf or cup a waxy white orchid in the hand. The atmosphere in the forest was very warm, very humid, very *green*. Greenness clung to her nostrils. That and a kind of primeval woodiness. It seemed to come not so much from the forest giants as the preponderance of enormously thick vines that hung down from the treetops like giant ropes.

Tarzan would have had the time of his life here, Eve smiled to herself and began fanning her heated face with her wide-brimmed straw hat. Her whole body was dewed with sweat, it was that humid. So pervasive was the atmosphere she felt if she stood in place she, too, would start sprouting ferns and the beautiful epiphytic orchids that gave this ancient holy place its special atmosphere. Some of the most beautiful orchids, the lavender, the purple, the soft yellow, lime green, orange and white grew very high up cascading their strongly scented flowers in spectacular six-foot drifts.

The plant life was overwhelming. There were distinct layers of secondary trees, all thrusting ever upwards to the great energy source: the light. Tree ferns rivalled these saplings for height, spreading their great feathery crowns. Cycads abounded, luxuriant coiling vines, mosses, lichens, areas of the most extraordinary fungi, exotic fleshy white objects growing out of the rich dark humus. There wasn't a square inch that wasn't covered in plant life. From these plants medicines could be developed. The aborigines had known for thousands of years the curative, hallucinogenic and deadly properties of certain trees, plants and shrubs. They had developed their own oils and potions. This wondrous diverse plant life could be used for the benefit of man. Their project filled her with excitement, never more so than here in the great rainforest. It was a project she could believe in and run with.

Up ahead, dressed in similar fashion to herself, jeans and a bush shirt, his sleek dark head uncovered, Drew was in deep conversation with the ranger. They had arrived by charter flight that morning, booking into their bungalow-style resort before catching up with the tour she herself had organised. Behind her, fascinated by the great size of the staghorns and elkhorns was Jack, who Eve now regarded as a friend. Jack had sent her copious material assembled by his staff and somehow Eve had managed to wade through it, always a quick study, absorbing a great deal of information in a very short time. Something that pleased Jack enormously, so he began to see himself as mentor, she his disciple. Even Drew, who Eve had found worked longer and harder than any of his staff, had taken time off to congratulate her. Though she would never had believed it if someone had suggested it that first day, an inner communication had developed between them that had a depth far beyond the spoken word. Although in a sense Drew Forsythe, through the sheer strength and vibrancy of his personality, had invaded what Eve thought of as her private space, it had been a truly exciting and rewarding experience. She was, she realised, beginning to lose her "fears" about him.

It was astonishing in its way. Years and years of building defences. A few short weeks to knock them down.

Fifteen minutes on, Drew and the ranger came back to her, the ranger responding to Jack's excited call.

"How's it going?" Drew allowed his dark eyes to rest on her lovely heat-slicked skin, that somehow contrived to give her a very sexy look. Her high cheekbones were touched with peach bloom, her eyes as fresh and green as the leaves, gold hair pulled up and away from her face. Her hairline, like his, was dewed with sweat. She looked a vastly different girl from the one he had first laid eyes on. More alive. More vibrant. Above all, relaxed, as though inside of her emotional fronds were unfurling.

"It would take a couple of lifetimes to see all this," she said, raising her arms to encompass the green world around them.

"And we're in for another adventure," he said lightly, "Gary is taking us back through the forest margin where all the butterflies hang out. The lantana there grows in great sprawling masses. Apparently the butterflies just love the nectar. They get drunk on it."

"That would be something to see." Eve glanced

briefly at her watch. "Don't forget you have your appointment at two-thirty."

He nodded. "And time gets away. Look at Jack. Isn't he in his element."

Well ahead of them now, Jack was enthusiastically pointing out a rainforest phenomenon known as cauliflory where flowers developed all over the trunks and the thick branches of the trees. The forest giant he was admiring was decorated with large bunches of white flowers for easily fifty or sixty feet of the giant trunk.

"I've enjoyed this trip enormously." Eve gave a sigh of pure satisfaction. "The whole feel of the place, the essence. No wonder Mrs. Garratt is a great lover of the land. And its our job to convince her we mean it no harm."

"Of course not."

Drew smiled and touched her shoulder. "Better move on, I suppose. I'd like to get a bite to eat before I meet with Will Dawson. I need him on site to reopen our old copper and gold mine at Mount Maratta."

Resigned to the fact it was time to go, Eve moved along the narrow track startled and delighted by the abrupt flight of a brilliant blue, orange and scarlet bird. It darted out of a giant fig, throwing a brilliant splash of colour in the green gloom before becoming invisible again in the dense leaves.

"What was that? A kingfisher?" Eve turned a rapt face to him, throwing out a hand. In the next instant she was caught up from behind, her shock enormous as Drew's strong arms locked around her dragging her back against him. "Lord, that was close!" His tone was uncharacteristically harsh.

Eve couldn't cover up. She couldn't even move. To

be in his arms paralysed her. Didn't he realise one of his hands was almost caressing her breast?

She couldn't seem to catch her breath as multiple sensations began to whip her round, tearing at her flesh like sharp little hooks. She was beginning to have feelings. *Such feelings* that had never been there before. Feelings like she was dissolving in a mix of raw longing and terror. She could smell the wonderful masculine scent of him, feel his clean breath brush her skin, the warmth of his flesh, thighs and strong legs. She couldn't handle this any more than she could staunch the violent flow of emotion. She wasn't accustomed to hot rushes of feeling. She who had been so numb for so long.

Drew, too, felt the fiery jolt of their close body contact. Shocked, as desire cut into him with the sharp thrust of a knife. Experienced as he was, he was fighting the compulsive urge to run his hands over the exquisite contours of her breasts, so clearly visible through her light clingy top. He had glimpsed this urge in him before. The urge to touch her. This young woman who was known and unknown to him. This clever girl as innocent as a novice. This Eve who for some reason was weeping inside.

He gave a brief laugh that seemed to work. "Even in this wonderful place there are hazards," he pointed out, releasing her before she bolted like a wild thing. "That plant you almost touched is the Stinging Tree. See the leaves and stems? Those stiff little hairs are full of poison. They break off at the slightest touch, injecting the skin. The result is a lot of pain and effects that can last for up to a month. As it happens, I need you on deck."

"I'm sorry. I didn't know." Eve shuddered in a kind of release.

The effort she made to appear normal after that mo-

ment of unbearable intimacy was touching and gallant.
It made him admire her. "I didn't hurt you, did I?"

"No." She dropped her eyes. Even more terrible, his
protective grasp had opened up some great cavern in her
letting in brilliant light.

"I know what we'll do." His beautiful dark eyes almost embraced her. "I'll walk ahead and you follow me.
That's right." He glanced back at her with approval.
"By the way, you missed an amethyst python a few
yards back."

Spontaneous in her reaction, Eve pitched forward to
clasp him around the waist. "What a horrible time to
tell me."

"I like it when you go all feminine." He grinned at
her, little brackets of amusement at the side of his disturbing mouth. "You can hang on until we get out of
here, if you like."

"I can't believe what a tease you are," Eve said. Then
miraculously, with a smile, "All right. I will."

On the forest margins they delayed for ten minutes
watching the gorgeous display of butterflies that flitted
in great numbers in and out of the great masses of flowering pink lantana in a kaleidoscope of colour and beating wings. Introduced from South America, the plant had
gone wild in the tropics, dominating the edges of the
forest in near-impenetrable towering cascades. Glorious
iridescent blue Ulysses delighted the eye, spectacular red
Lacewings, common jezebels with their vivid under-
sides, orange cruisers, the giant male Birdwing with its
eight-inch wing span. They were there. Too fragile. So
beautiful. "For some reason the birds leave them
alone," Gary, their guide explained. "Funny that, when
most birds hunt all manner of insects."

"Maybe it has something to do with the rapidity of their flight," Drew suggested. "The zigzag pattern."

"Maybe as beautiful as they are they don't taste so good." Eve smiled, her big straw hat shading her green eyes. Such happiness was spreading through her it scared her.

"Well, the spiders love them," their guide answered laconically. "It's hot, isn't it?" He ran a hand through his thick thatch of hair staring up at a cloudless peacock blue sky. "I wouldn't be surprised if we didn't have a corker of a late storm."

While Drew went off to his meeting and Jack took the opportunity to visit a friend, Eve walked to the village to do some sightseeing and maybe a little shopping. Even in late February with one minor cyclone after another forming in the Coral Sea, holding for a few days then mercifully blowing out to sea, she found the whole experience tremendously exciting. Born and bred in subtropical Brisbane still hadn't prepared her for the extraordinary brilliance of the landscapes north of Capricorn, the marvellous juxtaposition of the sea, the wonder of the Great Barrier Reef, the luxuriant jungles and river valleys.

No predatory tigers had stalked them in the rainforest but up here the armoured monsters that had survived the dinosaurs, the crocodiles, made their presence felt in rivers and creeks. Then again much of the atmosphere had to do with the volatile mix of races, the Italians who had made such a tremendous contribution to the sugar industry, the Spaniards, the Greeks, her own people of British stock, the Scandinavians, the Yugoslavs, the Chinese and the descendants of the Kanakas cruelly blackbirded in the previous century from their

Melanesian homes to work the sugar fields. Not so visible, seeming always dwelling on the fringe, were the original inhabitants of the continent, the aborigines like dark gentle souls moving in and out of the larger society waiting for the day when there would be full recognition of their rights.

The light, too, was mystical, magical, rolling over the lush landscape, the endless variety of greens lit by all the glory of the flowering trees and shrubs. No wonder so many artists came to live here, Eve thought. It would be a kind of ecstasy to be surrounded by so many landscapes, seascapes, and subjects to paint.

The tropics was a place where life *seethed*. Even the birds shrieked in abandon, not hiding themselves as they did in the forest but extraordinarily visible and tame. Eve had expected a flock of brilliantly enamelled lorikeets to take to the wing as she neared them but they remained in place picking the choicest grass seeds.

For an hour or more she wandered around the village, admiring the arts and crafts that were on display, visiting a marvellous little boutique that specialised in resort clothes and glowing hand-painted sarongs. Just the thing for around the pool. This thrill of happiness was new to her. Working for Drew Forsythe had opened up a new world. In a way it was like a thread of destiny. An unbreakable thread, it seemed. The more she tried to remain inside her own skin the more she was drawn to him. There was something utterly captivating about him as tough and masculine as he undoubtedly was. A charm, an animation, the dry deep vein of humour that made everybody laugh. She had never laughed with her old boss at Pearce Musgrave. The occasion had never arisen.

Complete with a few purchases, she was returning to the bus that would take her back to their resort when she noticed a frail-looking, beautifully dressed, elderly lady having trouble with her frisky little King Charles spaniel. Always ready to come to a needy person's aid, Eve quickened her pace. The lady, short silver hair, dressed all in white, white linen trousers and a loose matching shirt, was speaking firmly to the exuberant little dog, trying to call it to order.

"Stay, Suki," she said. "Stay."

Suki had no such intention. He had come into the village with his mistress, now he intended to have a good time. Although the lady tightened her hold on its lead, it scampered free, racing merrily along the colourful lined footpath before deciding to check out across the road.

Swiftly Eve let her parcels fall to the ground. Cars, mostly four-wheel drives, weren't all that frequent but one could turn the corner at any time.

"Suki, Suki, come back. It's not safe," Suki's owner called out in distress.

"Don't worry, I'll get him," Eve flung over her shoulder, and sprinted after the little dog, whistling to it as she went.

The spaniel turned in swift acknowledgment, seemed about to obey, then decided it preferred the game.

Eve pressed on, blond hair whipping, wings on her feet. In the heat she was wearing a pink camisole and white shorts, her long legs flashing as she overtook the little dog who was running from right to left and back again as though leading her a merry dance was half the fun.

When she finally caught him, scooping him up under her arm, applause broke out from the customers who were enjoying coffee under the shade of fringed umbrellas on the pavement.

"My dear, I can't begin to thank you," the lady said when Eve returned the spaniel to her waiting arms. "Oh, you are a naughty dog, Suki."

It was said in such loving tones it activated a soft satisfied rumble from Suki.

"So full of life and they love a game." Eve smiled and reached out a hand to stroke a black silky ear.

"Could I ask you to join me in a cup of coffee?" the lady who was beautifully spoken with elegant narrow features asked.

"That would be lovely." Eve was surprised but quite agreeable. She had debated enjoying an iced coffee by herself but decided it would wait until she got back to the resort. Now this distinguished elderly lady who somehow looked quite sad had asked her to join her. She bent to retrieve her purchases.

"Perhaps Sugar and Spice, over there," Eve's new-found friend suggested. "We can share a table under the umbrella and I'll be able to secure this little menace."

Of course, when you thought about it. It *had* to be. The exact part of the world. The trained voice. The classic expensive clothes. The distinguished stage bearing.

"Eve Copeland, Mrs. Garratt." Eve smiled back, the kindness and gentleness she had always shown to her mother in her clear green eyes. She felt a little regret their meeting had happened this way. This was the woman they desperately needed to sell to them and although it was a marvellous opportunity to speak, Eve felt loathe to intrude on Elizabeth Garratt's simple uncomplicated pleasure.

"Now how does anyone as young as yourself know me?" Elizabeth Garratt asked with considerable surprise, looking back into Eve's face and liking what she saw.

"I've seen many photographs of you over the years."
Eve smiled. "Alas, not one of your memorable perform-
ances."

"You must be a very observant girl," Elizabeth
Garratt was moved to say. "All those photographs were
taken many years ago."

"You haven't changed." Which was true. Suddenly
Eve needed to be completely honest. "Also, it's part of
my training."

"You must tell me." Mrs. Garratt relaxed in her chair.
There was a sweet smile in her still lovely blue eyes,
her short naturally curly silver hair blowing gently in the
breeze. "I lead a rather lonely life these days," she faltered briefly, "especially since I lost my husband, my
dear companion."

Eve knew it was an inadequate response but on im-
pulse she leaned forward and gently squeezed the
woman's fingers.

"Oh, you know?" Elizabeth Garratt looked into Eve's
eyes, finding them sympathetic and safe.

"Yes." Eve lowered her voice. "I lost my mother a
few years ago. There's not a day I don't feel the pain."

"You understand quite a lot for your age, I think."
Elizabeth Garratt gave another sad little smile then made
a visible effort to brighten. "Now what would you like
to eat with your coffee? I hope you have the time. This
is a little treat for me, as well. I've never seen you before
so you must be up here on holidays?"

"A few days." Eve flushed a little uncertain how to
handle this.

"Lovely!" Elizabeth Garrett nodded several times
then gestured to the young man who was serving at the
tables. "You might be able to find the time to visit me
if it's not too much of a bore to visit an old lady. My

home has a truly magnificent view. Perhaps we could have lunch.''

There was nothing else for it, Eve thought. As soon as we've eaten I have to make a full confession. Not confession. She'd done nothing wrong. On the other hand Elizabeth Garratt was very plainly a woman who could be hurt, might think Eve had somehow engineered their meeting. A bit unlikely when one thought about it, but a touchy situation. Clearly Elizabeth Garratt had taken to her and Eve had no intention of abusing her trust.

When Drew returned to the resort late afternoon, he went in search of Eve and found her in the swimming pool. He stood looking for a while, watching her cutting smoothly through the turquoise water in a very stylish freestyle tumble turn fifty metres. Not only was her action stylish, it was *fast*. Which really didn't surprise him. She had an athletic look about her and those long legs. He spent a bit of time looking at them he suddenly realised. Hell, he was a man. No, more than that. It was Eve he was looking at. Eve with her mystery.

But the heat! The blue sky was smouldering and there were dark purple storm clouds massing over the glittering expanse of the sea. Even the air was thrumming with electricity.

''Isn't it a bit hot for that?'' He went to the shallow end of the pool where she emerged, and gave her a hand out, conscious their joined hands fairly crackled and spat. In her clothes he had thought her too thin. Now in an emerald green Lycra one-piece he realised she had a perfect figure. Model slender, beautiful sloping shoulders, delicate breasts, naturally indented waist, long lean thighs and those racehorse legs.

"Have you missed anything?" she suddenly asked, more tart than provocative.

"Evie, Evie, you're full of challenge," he replied. "To be honest, I always thought you a mite too thin. Now you look darned near perfect. Anyway, it's too hot for our first little spat. Come over to the shade and cool off."

Under the swaying palms did look idyllic. One part of her wanting to race away. The other desperately wanting to stay. The consequences of falling in love with Drew Forsythe would be swift and severe. She didn't want it to happen.

"Did your meeting go okay?" she asked, leading him to her recliner where she had stashed her beach bag and multicoloured straw hat.

Drew shrugged. "Well, he started putting up objections at first. I thought he might, but I think I addressed all his concerns. I'll see him again before we go. What about you? What did you do with yourself?"

"You're not going to believe this," Eve said.

"Let me guess. You ran into an old admirer?"

"No. Far more significant."

"Evie. Now you've got me worried." He sat in a chair watching her lazily while she towelled off then wrapped herself in her new sarong, a brilliant blend of sea colours that made her green eyes blaze.

"Nothing to be worried about."

"Everything you do is safe, Eve." It sounded like a gentle taunt.

"You make me sound very dull."

He put up his hand to a drinks waiter in the distance, ordered them both a long frosted drink. "On the contrary. I think you're real cool." He flicked her a sidelong smile. "Tell me all about it."

"I'm determined to despite the teasing." Eve stretched out on the recliner, scooping up her hair and twisting it into a knot. "I met Mrs. Garratt."

He leaned towards her, his relaxed expression sharpening. "I'm sure I told you we were going to work out a strategy first?"

"Now, now, don't sound like the boss," she soothed. "It was a happy chance meeting."

"Really?" He gave her a long look. "How did you engineer that?"

Eve's casual pose stiffened. "Look, I was hoping you'd hear me through."

He took her hand for a moment, thoroughly undermining her. "Fire away, Evie. I have the time."

"So that's how it happened," Eve finished a good ten minutes later having been directed to let him in on every word. "We parted the best of friends. I'm having lunch with her tomorrow. I was tempted to ask if you could come along but decided on the softly softly approach as agreed.

"Elizabeth Garratt is prepared to at least listen to what we have to say. She told me about all her battles with developers. The battles she finally won. But she had to admit TCR has an excellent track record for up-front consultations. On that basis she'll listen. I'll start the ball rolling and you of course have to take over. It's a start."

"Bet on it." Drew gave a low quiet whistle. "We'll go over all of this at dinner. It won't require much. You know your stuff." Eve, he had found in a very short time, was excellent at smoothing paths.

Jack decided not to join them for dinner. He'd had a long lunch with a friend and thought enough was enough, but he was enormously pleased to hear Eve had not only made contact with the reclusive Elizabeth

Garratt but had even secured entree to her home. No mean feat if one was to believe all one read.

Towards seven, Drew picked her up at her beachfront bungalow two up from his own, escorting her along the lantern-lit paths flanked by lush gardens that gave off the scent of gardenia and ginger blossom, to the main building where the restaurant was housed. Once as he lifted away an overhanging palm frond his hand rested very briefly on her shoulder, long fingers curving around her bare nape. What are you doing to me? Eve thought in alarm. Didn't he know the sensations his slightest touch could provoke? She couldn't ignore it but it was vital it all went away. One step, one tiny step over the boundary and it would be impossible to return. It was with a sense of relief Eve made her way out of the intoxicating darkness into the pool of light from the main building.

The Fountain Room was beginning to fill with guests but she just knew they would get a top table overlooking the beach. A copper moon was riding a black velvet sky but the air out in the garden had been sulphurous with the continuing threat of a late storm. There were smiles all round as they walked to their table, people looking at them in a certain way. If most didn't actually know who Drew was he had such an air of glamour he had to be someone. Maybe a movie star.

"This okay?" Drew asked when they were seated.

Eve glanced over her shoulder, her hair swinging. "I would probably say it's the top table."

"Ah, well, the owner knows me," Drew mocked. "Now what are we going to have? Seafood, right?" He shot her a smiling glance, picking up the wine list.

"Something light. I'm not used to a lot of food."

"Hey, you could do with a few pounds more."

"It's not what you said this afternoon. I thought I was perfect."

The deep attractive creases appeared in his lean cheeks. "The point is a few more pounds wouldn't show. Things should be easier for you and Ben now, shouldn't they?"

"I bless the day you hired me." Eve stroked the yellow heart of a frangipani in the small flower arrangement.

"Do you?" His eyes moved over her face, dipped to her breast. She was wearing a simple slip dress in a deep shade of violet which the grace of her body made elegant. Already her skin had picked up a pale golden colour.

The princess behind her tangled web of thorns, he thought. Breach it at your peril.

Eve nearly knocked over her wineglass at what she read in his eyes.

"What's that look supposed to mean?"

"Like the rest of us, Eve, you give out little messages."

"Such as?"

In the soft glow from the table candle her eyes had gone darkest emerald.

"Something about me still troubles you."

"I don't think it wise to get personal."

He saw the guardedness that entered her face. "Except we're human. And, Evie, though I know it's the last thing you want, we're attracted to each other."

Suddenly it was out, the secret that ran deep.

"You must be used to that." She tried to dismiss it with a gesture.

"And you're the expert on men."

Eve thought she was safe for quite a while. Over dinner of succulent scallops on the shell followed by roast lobster with a mesclun salad they discussed the details of the proposal Eve would take to Elizabeth Garratt, allowing her to consider the project as a whole. If on reflection she found it acceptable Drew would take over the negotiations with Eve as the executive assistant who had made the initial impression. The atmosphere which had become quick-fire and businesslike was suddenly dispelled over coffee.

"So what about it, Evie." Drew spoke satirically, very smooth and confident. "Can we pick up on our conversation?"

She met his challenging dark eyes.

"I have a bit of a problem with breaking the rules."

"I can see that." He gave her a half smile. "Is having dinner with your boss breaking the rules? A divorced man, to boot. I take it that's a big strike against me."

"How could it be?" Eve took another sip of her drink. "A lot of people get divorced every day. In any case, it has nothing to do with me."

"I thought at the beginning it almost enraged you." He gave her a dubious smile.

"No." She shook her blond head.

"*Yes,* Evie, you were very mistrustful. In fact, you were positively looking for something to blame me for."

She saw that it was useless to deny it. "I suppose it might have been something to do with my past. Ben and I are the children of divorce."

He nodded. "And I sympathize. But you feel in most cases it's the guy's fault?"

"Isn't it?" she asked with more bitterness than she intended.

He stared at her, looking very serious and analytical.

"Under your cool exterior there's a very angry little girl. But you can't right the wrongs by getting mad at *all* men. I tried very hard to make *my* marriage work."

"Please, Drew." She didn't want to discuss his marriage. She didn't want to think of him in love with another woman. God, was she mad!

"Why are you frightened of this conversation?" he questioned her.

"What it could lead to." She didn't care if for a moment her panic showed. Already he was looming far too large in her life.

"Look at me, Evie." There was an echo of tenderness in his deep voice.

"I want you to be my *boss,*" Eve protested, staring fixedly out the window.

"The difficulty is our relationship has progressed beyond that point. Is it wrong for me to want to get to know you?" Get to know everything there is to know about you, he thought.

"Drew." She turned her head, looking far from her composed self. "I must tell you I'll *never* be the one to get hurt."

"And it will happen if you allow yourself to fall in love?" he asked a little harshly.

"I saw my mother's devastation," Eve said. "Not for weeks and months. I saw it day after day for *years*. In my experience men don't allow themselves to get as deeply involved as women. They have their *professional* lives. Their big careers. I made a decision early on not to expose my heart in the same way as my mother."

"Poor little Evie," he said gently. "So you haven't had any serious involvement with a man?"

"For very obvious reasons." Sexual hostility flooded

her. "I'm going to act as a man does. I'm going to place my career first."

"You don't want marriage, children?" he continued, still in that quiet voice, his dark eyes enigmatic.

"I didn't say that." She shook her head. "I mean I don't want to be utterly, completely in a man's power."

"The worst fate. Have you had any sexual relationship at all?"

"Come on." Evie made a fiery elegant little gesture. "That's an extraordinarily private question."

"And I don't ask it lightly," he stated back at her, noting her faint trembling. *"Have you?"*

I can retreat now. Right inside my head. "I have no intention of telling you. I've had one or two little romances."

"But you turn off when your friends want to turn into your lovers?"

"I don't have a mania for sex, Drew," she drawled. "I can take it or leave it." Which was probably true.

"Obviously you haven't met the person who can release all that hostility and anger," he ventured.

"Love transforms, Evie. I've seen the light of love in your face when you talk about your brother. I know you'd do anything to help him. But one day he's going to become fully independent. He's going to find the right woman, fall in love and marry. Start a family of his own."

"Surely you haven't formed the notion it's not my great wish," Eve said with more than a touch of frost.

"But you want the opposite for yourself?"

Why, oh why, did he want to figure her out? Couldn't he see danger lay thick around them? "Drew, I love working for you," she said. "I admire and respect you as my boss. Forgive me if I see you in my private life as one great big threat.''

''Can't you tell me why?'' He looked deep into her eyes.

''You damned well know why,'' she answered in a taut voice.

''Do you think I'm looking for an affair?''

The psychoanalysis continued. ''You can't deny you don't have them?''

''Many of my friends are women,'' he freely admitted. ''Women are glorious creatures. Strong, capable, possessed of great warmth and compassion. The women of my family on both sides were like that. I draw repeatedly on memories of my mother. I adored her. She was so brave, so full of fight, but she lost the battle with cancer.''

She brushed one side of her long blond hair from her face. ''I'm sorry, Drew. I'm sure she was a wonderful woman, but your father married again.'' A pause. ''A much younger model,'' she added with deep irony.

''Women are drawn to powerful figures.''

''Your stepmother loves him?'' she challenged. Whatever the story, Eve *knew* at some level Lady Forsythe was a little in love with Drew. And who could blame her?

''People strike bargains and accommodations every day, Evie. You know that,'' he answered reasonably, keeping his own temper down. ''Susan feels deeply about my father. She was devastated when she lost the child. A lot of women go after status, a privileged lifestyle. Men, too. It's happened all through history.''

''I'm sorry.'' Eve's little smile was sad and apologetic. ''But, Drew, you *started* all this.''

''Admitted, and I don't want to make you miserable.

I'm trying to draw you out. There might be a little bit of pain but you can see it might help."

"Be a psychiatrist. Be whatever you want to be." She half expected to feel the wetness of tears on her cheeks. "Are you trying to tell me you *care?*"

"I'll care if you *let* me," he said quietly.

"I'm not ready for someone like you, Drew. I'll never be ready," she said.

They were silent on the way back to the bungalows, moving swiftly along the maze of pathways in an effort to beat the storm that was now imminent. There was no sign of the moon and stars. The cloud build up was complete, lowering over them, menacing. The great fronds of the tall palms whipped in the strong blustery wind that was coming off the sea laden with salt and a peculiar fragrance like incense. For a moment Eve thought she would be swept off her feet, but Drew grasped her around the waist, telling her with some urgency to keep her head down. The flowering shrubs, the oleanders, were taking a battering, tossing their branches right in their path.

"Hell," Drew muttered as he compelled her up the short flight of steps to her bungalow. "I just hope this isn't Cyclone Nell coming to life." Nell had been stationary well off the coast.

A great jagged bolt of lightning flashed across the sky and buried itself in the earth. Another minute and it was followed by a violent clap of thunder that made Eve jump.

"Go in. Get shelter," Drew shouted above the din, adrenalin tingling through his veins. Despite the danger, storms had always filled him with a sense of awe and exhilaration.

No so Eve. One of Ben's closest friends from his school days had been killed by a lightning strike when he was out with his father on their boat. For years after, the boy's mother had gone slightly crazy until she settled into a dull acceptance. He had been, after all, an only child. Ben still felt a strong personal loss.

Inside the bungalow Eve turned on lights, trying to tighten her hold over her high emotion.

"Evie?" Drew turned to give her a concerned look. Eve, the cool, the clever, the competent. She looked a little strange, her green eyes brilliant. "You're all right, aren't you?"

For answer Eve closed her eyes as another flash of lightning seared the sky and lit up the bungalow. "I *hate* electrical storms. They're so dangerous."

"You must be used to them living in Brisbane all your life."

"They never used to worry me," Eve said tightly. "At one time I actually found them exciting but a friend of Ben's was killed by a lightning strike. It was in all the papers. A few years back. He was out on the bay with his father. They almost made it back."

"That's tragic. I seem to remember it." Drew lifted his eyes as the lights of the bungalow flickered and dimmed. "There are some candles inside the kitchen cupboard. We'd better get them out just in case."

"Yes." For a moment Eve didn't move she was so shaken.

"You sit down. I'll get them," Drew said, moving quickly to do just that.

Rain was lashing down, drumming on the roof of the bungalow, sweeping across its small veranda and rattling the windows. Eve saw one was half open, but she didn't want to walk across to it the lightning was so bad.

"Another ten minutes and this will be over." Drew comforted her, moving now to shut the window against the driving rain. "Even if the lights go out we have the candles."

Eve picked up a cushion, hugged it to herself. "I'm glad you're with me. This is the worst storm I've ever experienced."

"It's pretty volcanic at that," Drew was forced to admit. "But it poses no real threat. The real threat is if the cyclone comes in. They're just so damned destructive."

He had barely finished speaking when a quite terrifying burst of thunder threatened to shake the timber supports of the bungalow.

"God, this is awful!" Eve pressed her hands to her ears. She was trembling. Doing damage to herself. She had to stop. It wasn't only fear of the lightning she had to control. It was fear of showing her vulnerable core. She had endured a lifetime of thunderstorms. A lot of them she had even enjoyed. She would get through this. But the assault of the rain on the roof was like some massive bombardment, that and the thunder that rolled and cracked.

The lights dulled and as her nerves jumped in shock, abruptly went out.

"Drew?"

"It's all right." There was no trace of anything but the utmost calm in his voice.

"God, I don't know what's the matter with me tonight. I'm being silly I know."

"We're all afraid of something."

"Except *you*." Maybe it was the wine that sent a rush to her brain.

"Don't deliberately play with fire, Eve," he warned. Squat candles in their storm shades flared into life, spreading a golden illumination over his handsome down-bent face. His physical presence filled the room but for all his quietness he, too, looked tense as though the turbulence of the atmosphere was affecting him, as well.

"I can't always be careful," Eve protested, thinking the tension was almost visible. "If you're so wise, you should have left me on my own."

"I suspect it's because right now you need me." He came towards her, so tall and vital, Eve felt a powerful tide of inevitability. You pay for everything, she thought wildly. Terrible mistakes have terrible penalties.

"Lord, Evie, what's your problem," he groaned, on edge but still retaining his good humour. "It's one hell of a time for a seduction surely?" Yet there were little tongues of fire in his dark, dark eyes.

"That's good, because I think we'd both be *very, very* sorry." Eve couldn't have been more aware of her own emotional fragility.

"You think it might interfere with your career?" He sounded both amused and challenging.

"I wouldn't be the first woman who had to quit."

He looked her over, a twist to his sensuous mouth. "You're assuming a lot, aren't you, curled up on that sofa? You're not ready for a *tiny* affair let alone what I might or might not be considering."

Tightness gathered in her throat. "Please, Drew, let it go at that. I know I sound awful."

"Actually you sound like a paragon of virtue." There

was wryness and a certain toughness in his voice. "Just be quiet now and everything will be okay."

He moved determinedly to the window, looking out at the tempest, closing his eyes for a moment against another brilliant flash of electricity-spitting lightning. The rain, if anything, was coming down harder, the fronds of the golden canes outside the window thrashing from side to side.

When he finally turned back to Eve he found her paper white, tears sliding down her face. His heart melted and his own edgy feelings fell away. "Evie, Evie." He had the tremendous urge to kiss the tears away. "This place has been built to withstand cyclones. "We're quite safe."

"I don't like it all the same." She dashed her hand across her face in self-disgust.

He knelt before her and took her hands. "What is it? What's really wrong?"

At his keen perception, as though he knew her so well, she threw back her head wordlessly, exposing the clean line of her chiselled chin and throat. Where was her famous detachment now? Her feelings for him were so new, so threatening, they rubbed her raw.

Drew didn't hesitate. He sat down beside her, drawing her into his arms. "You've got a lot of tears locked up inside, haven't you?" He swept her hair off her face, looking deep into her eyes.

For the space of that moment there was no sound. The fury of the storm had opened the floodgate, now it was silenced as Drew, his heart leaping, his body full of desperate hungers that had never been assuaged, bent his head and kissed her lovely passionate mouth. As he always knew he would. Fate had placed her in his life.

Somehow without knowing it, he lifted her across his

knees so her head was thrown back against the crook of his arm. She wasn't cold or resistant at all. She was a boneless, yielding, beautiful *woman* creature, her mouth dissolving under the heat of his like the tears on her cheeks or the rain that overwhelmed the landscape.

Surrendering to this hot aching tide, his hand slid from the curve of her chin, across her shoulder and down the satin flesh of her breast. So slight, her body so young and taut, she had no need of a bra and his fingers met the peaks of her breasts nuzzling them until she moaned in his arms. It was a miracle. A shared experience, passionate yet poignant. He had never known a woman so wonderful to kiss, to touch. He bent his head to her breast, pushing the top of her slip dress off her shoulder, his hand sliding down over a delicate hip, seeking the hem of her dress. No haste, no violence, but an ecstasy of tenderness. Eve was so vulnerable. He couldn't bear to frighten her. But his hunger was merciless.

To Eve, almost fainting at the onslaught of high sensuality, her body trembling under his exploratory hands, it was like being *possessed*. Something new was running in her veins burning like molten lava.

*Desire*. The fall of fire. When she had wanted only to escape it.

He was so much more than a brilliant lover. Sensitive, imaginative, passionately romantic. He was a magician. Or a great artist.

She couldn't believe how far she had come. Dressing in such a flimsy dress, explaining it away as the heat. Every defence she had put up over the years crumbled before the triumphant male. Treacherous feelings engulfed her. Drunk on a kiss. Yet she couldn't stand not to open her mouth to him.

His hand moved across her lace briefs, about to *find*

her, invade her in an eye's blink, only a flash of her old resistance radiated up and out. Senses swimming, candlelight leaping over her exposed flesh, Eve turned her body so violently she would have fallen to the floor only Drew caught her back.

"I can't." Her voice shook, her heart shuddering in her chest. Really, it was sad she was so messed up.

"You can't what?" His voice was slurred as though he, too, was affected.

"I don't want this." Eve sat straight, pulling the thin strap of her dress back up her arm and onto her shoulder, acutely conscious her tightly budded nipples peaked against the violet fabric.

"That wasn't my impression, Evie," he said with some mockery, kissing the back of her neck. "I won't apologise because I made you aware of your own sensuality. You surely can't think I was about to rape you?" His voice matched his suave look.

"Don't joke about it," she said shortly, her emotions ricocheting between a fierce longing and terror.

"Let's get something straight." His hands found her smooth warm arms and closed on them. "You must know I'm falling in love with you?"

At his words Eve's heart fluttered wildly, like a bird beating its wings against a cage. Could it possibly be true, or just the usual male tactic to get a woman into bed? Charming women was a way of life for him. The expert rushing her into a headlong arousal.

"Hey, it isn't a bad thing!" he interrupted her thoughts wryly. "What's important for me to know is, are you a virgin?"

Eve's cheeks flamed scarlet, her voice overemotional

even to her own ears. "You're wondering about that, are you?"

"I sense you are but I'm not insulting you, Evie." He tucked a long golden strand of hair behind her ear. So certain of her. Dangerous. Mesmerising. "I want to take care of you," he murmured seductively. "I've had my affairs. I've been married. Now I'm looking for a serious involvement. With *you*. A deep involvement. With you. I don't think you're as unwilling as you try to make out."

No, I'm just sabotaging my chance to be happy. Eve bowed her head, shattered. "I don't know. I *can't* know." She was forced to admit her ambivalence. "I'm only certain of one thing. TCR won't be big enough for both of us. I'll be the one who has to go."

"You think I'm likely to fire you?"

He seemed to be teasing her. Thrilling her. Dominating her. When she cared not a jot for domination. "Why not? You dumped your wife," she retaliated sharply, then could have bitten her tongue. All this anger and hostility was fed by old fears and confusions, a rising frenzy of desire that had brought her shockingly alive.

"That's rubbish," he answered with magnificent disdain. "And it's not *you*, Evie. It's your past that's eating you up. You won't put me off, whatever you say. I'm very serious about you. I've had as many go-nowhere affairs as I can take."

All her senses overstrung, Eve made another attempt to pierce his armour. "Your wife isn't even out of your life. She's still tied to you," she accused, watching his handsome face harden.

"That's absurd, Eve, and I don't need it."

Eve gave a little jangled laugh. "It's *not*. I saw her.

I *saw* Susan. She's virtually the same age as you. You mightn't set out to have women falling in love with you but they can't seem to stop themselves.''

"Aren't I lucky.'' He spoke with bitter irony. "I have most things I need, Eve, but I don't have *the* woman to love.''

She looked back at him with blazing, don't-mess-with-me eyes, swallowing up her face, green as lakes. "Is this a ploy to get me into bed?''

He lifted a hand to his temple, rubbed it. "I might live for the moment, Evie, but no. I'm not perfect, sure, but I don't go around covering every woman with kisses.''

"Why did you leave your wife?'' Eve asked more quietly.

"Why?'' He answered with a touch of grief. "I couldn't stand it any more.''

"You must have loved her to marry her.'' Eve kept her eyes trained on his face. It was important for her to understand.

He considered that for perhaps the umpteenth time. "None of us know what real love is until it hits. I *thought* I was in love with Carol. That's all I can say. She's very attractive and she can be good company. It took quite a while to accept she's fundamentally selfish. We discussed having a family before we married. She smiled sweetly but concealed her true feelings. She didn't want children at all. Not at any point. She swore she was off the pill well into our marriage but I discovered quite by chance she wasn't. Her upset when I confronted her was real enough. She wept buckets. But she told me then what she should have told me before. She didn't want children to disturb the harmony of our lives. She shuddered at the very thought of going through a pregnancy. I softened at once. I thought it might have been quite natural fears, and I could help her over them, but it was her *figure* she was worried about. I had her mother talk to her. Her doctor. But in the end it became clear to all of us. Carol was simply being herself.''

"So you couldn't get her to change her mind?'' Eve listened, dismayed. It all had the unmistakable ring of truth.

"As I said, I sure as hell tried,'' he rejoined flatly. ''I woke up too late to Carol's mercenary side. She may have wanted me but she wanted my perceived position and wealth more.''

"It must have wounded you, Drew,'' Eve said with sudden clarity.

"It did for a time. But not now. My life has taken a difference course since you came into it.''

Eve felt herself melt under the sensuous heat of his gaze. As his hand circled her nape languorously, she closed her eyes, opening her mouth to accept his kiss. It was slow, deep, full of sizzling passion but an almost unbearable tenderness, too. For a long moment her being merged with his. Was consumed. Whatever was between them, the unanswered questions, his lovemaking was wonderful!

# CHAPTER FIVE

THE acquisition of the Garratt land went through without a hitch. Sir David had returned from his trip to Japan and Indonesia where TCR had mining interests, the project, working name "Capricornia," had been accepted by the board. A big celebratory party was scheduled for the end of the month with many guests from government, the business and social world being invited, including Elizabeth Garratt who had surprised them all by deciding to come. Eve had sent a personal letter to accompany the gold-embossed invitation, which, Drew remarked privately, had swung it. Though he had met with Elizabeth Garratt several times when the dealing was on, she had insisted Eve be part of the group. She had come to look on Eve as a friend.

"We're kindred spirits," she told Drew, a teasing light in her blue eyes. "Even if you are irresistible to women."

Flattery indeed but Elizabeth Garratt drove a hard bargain, Drew found, earning for herself a private villa in the grounds of the proposed resort. She confided now she had locked herself away far too long. She planned to spend part of the year in the city if Eve could find her a suitable apartment. Which of course Eve did.

"Boy, have you come up in the world," Ben remarked, reading out her invitation. "Don't let it go to your head."

"As if I would."

"And what about the magnificent Drew?" Ben asked, a serious thread behind the teasing. "Face it, he's getting to be more than your boss."

Eve, who was sewing a button on his shirt, jabbed herself with the needle. "Damn!"

Ben laughed and passed her a box of tissues. "Is there something I should know?"

Eve smiled, the same loving smile she always gave him. "Calm down, brother, nothing's happening."

*"Yet,"* Ben answered wryly, "you're getting more beautiful every day. You've always had a look of your own. Very cool and classy even in clothes we know weren't good enough for you. But these days, you pack quite a punch."

"I need to look good. You know that."

"Especially when Drew is paying you a fortune," Ben said dryly.

"I think I deserve it. I work hard. Long hours. And I did close the Garrett deal. Well, Drew did, but I set it up."

Ben tapped his nails on the table. "One thing is certain. You've been developing lots of new interests since you met him. All these functions you're invited to. You've been photographed together at least four times. I wonder what the ex thinks of that?"

"Probably doesn't like it." Eve winced to herself.


As the days sped away Eve made the first move to find herself an evening dress. She'd never really had the occasion to dress up before joining TCR, much less the money. Now she was able to write off a large part of her wardrobe as a business expense. Ben wasn't the only one to get a kick out of her transformation. One glance from Drew's dark eyes was like being stroked all over with a velvety-soft brush. Suddenly she was a Woman. A woman moreover who needed a great dress for a big party. Lady Forsythe, who she had met only once and who didn't appear to recognise her, always looked fabulous. As everyone was going, even Drew's ex-wife and new high-profile partner, she had to hold her own.

Lisa, as usual, accompanied her on her shopping spree, almost as excited to choose Eve's outfits as if she were buying for herself. Finally they narrowed it down to three. Hand-beaded lilac lace in the very fashionable slip style, another a sequin and bead encrusted silk chiffon in a green that gave great depth to Eve's eyes, and classic black with diamanté.

"You'll have to pull out the jewels," Lisa said, rustling through the racks.

"What jewels?" Eve called from the cubicle, smoothing the lilac lace over her hips. One had to be in great shape for this kind of gear.

"A beaut pair of diamond earrings would do."

"Try rhinestones," Eve laughed.

"No, seriously, I have a pair I could lend you," Lisa the most generous of friends, said.

"I wouldn't take them, Lisa." Eve came out of the booth for inspection. "Thanks all the same. Imagine if I lost your twenty-first birthday present from your mum and dad."

"They're insured." Lisa shrugged that off. "You're going to a very formal party. I want you to look the goods."

In the end they all thought the green, Eve handing the garment to the boutique owner who gave her a beaming smile. "I must say I like your style, dear."

"She should have seen you a few months ago," Lisa

whispered in a joking aside. "Virgin to smart, sexy Vogue. I always said you could be a knockout."

Twenty minutes before her guests were due to arrive Susan Forsythe swept around the house checking on everything as she went. Her whole aim from day one had been to be the perfect wife. *Second* wife. But no matter how many times since she had become Lady Forsythe and played hostess at David's parties she always felt nervous and exposed to many critical eyes. Not that any of it showed. She could be as poised and confident as the rest of them. But so many of David's friends had been friends of the late Lady Forsythe. No one, it seemed, could possibly measure up to that great lady. She had been genuinely loved and respected. A portrait of her still hung in the living room. A very beautiful woman, Drew had his mother's wonderful eyes, fine, brilliant but melting, as though the person they belonged to was full of warmth and feeling. Susan would have liked to remove the portrait but that would have been viewed as treason.

The long skirt of her striking black evening dress rustled as she walked into the dining room, her radiant blue eyes sweeping the beautifully appointed buffet. The finest table linen, silverware, crystal. Two large silver swans held the floral arrangement. All white. Butterfly orchids, lilies, roses and carnations, their purity set off by the deep green of the assorted foliage. Nothing stuffy and overdone. Lovely fresh flowers, beautifully arranged. She desperately needed David to feel proud of her. Once a woman with an established career in public relations, she now devoted herself to making her husband's very busy life run smoothly. It was her primary aim in life, that, and trying to alleviate the stress that came with a big job. She felt honoured to be his wife. She had wanted their child so much. Part of him. Part of family. Part of—

Susan gave a profound sigh, conscious her thoughts weren't entirely centred on David. On the way upstairs to their bedroom she fingered her new necklace, the latest present from her husband, 18-carat yellow gold with a very modern and striking diamond pendant. It was a spectacular piece of jewellery and she had the looks to wear it.

It irked her considerably Carol Forsythe had been invited, if only because she and the highly successful Peter Morgan were an item. Carol no longer had a place in their life. The most self-centred young woman Susan had ever met. Drew was well rid of her. Everyone but everyone wanted to be the second Mrs. Drew Forsythe. Drew was—magic.

The one to definitely watch, strange as it seemed because she had no background to speak of, was his assistant Eve Copeland, from all accounts a very clever and competent girl with the same cool blond looks of a young Grace Kelly. Of course Eve Copeland was the one who had caught her in Drew's arms a certain day months ago, though Susan had pretended not to know her. Drew, being Drew, had been comforting her. But that was the day her feelings for him had changed, slipped into a new dimension. Privileged as her life now was, it wasn't all bliss.

"One hell of a place, isn't it?" Jamie whispered to Eve as they stood in the reception line. "I believe the present Lady Forsythe spent a couple of million making a few changes. Of course it was all Madelyn's style. She was worshipped in this city," Jamie remembered.

Then she must be a very hard act to follow, crossed

Eve's mind. Under a magnificent cut-glass chandelier in the entrance hall stood Sir David and Lady Forsythe receiving their guests. Eve had been introduced to Sir David on his return from overseas and found him courteous but slightly chilling, with a severe, rather preoccupied manner.

Certainly he was handsome, looking a good ten years younger than his acknowledged sixty-three. Silver wings added distinction to his still raven dark hair. Drew had a strong look of him, the lean height, the cast of features, but there the similarity ended. Sir David had little of his son's great charm of manner and the eyes so important to the whole arrangement of the face differed in colour and expression. Sir David's eyes were a piercing icy blue well in keeping with his personal style. Drew's were his mother's, as Eve was to find out.

Lady Forsythe looked stunning. It took a lot of money to look like that, Eve thought. The gown, hair, the ultra-pampered skin, the diamonds that sparkled at her ears and throat. Eve had never seen such a necklace. It was very modern in design and it went brilliantly with the formal black gown. She appeared in her element receiving all their guests. There was no sign of Drew.

When it was their turn to be greeted Sir David shot Eve one of his rapier glances, but complemented her on her appearance, surprisingly calling her by her Christian name. Jamie received an abrupt, ''Good evening, Foster.'' Once past their hosts Eve allowed her eye to roam all over the entrance hall. It certainly made a statement. Beautiful classical console, holding a glorious flower arrangement that must have cost a fortune, handsome gilded antique settee and chairs, magnificent carved rosewood stands holding tall Oriental vases of exquisite design. The floor was the traditional black and white marble, the divided staircase led to the painting-lined gallery above. To either side arched colonnades led to the main reception rooms.

Eve and Jamie followed the crowd, entering a very large living room that in turn led to what must be the library. She could see walls of books through leaded-glass doors and a huge yellow terrestrial globe within its timber stand. The living room was absolutely lovely furnished in apricots, peachy-pinks and yellows for the many deep sofas and the drapes with a harmonising print on the scatter of Louis-style armchairs. Beautiful gilded oval mirrors flanked the white marble fireplace. Over the mantel was a light-filled Impressionist painting, the far end of the room dominated by a nine-foot gleaming black Steinway. If Eve had asked, which she did later, she would have been told the piano belonged to the first Lady Forsythe who had been a very fine pianist and had given many a concert to raise funds for charity in this very room.

"I wonder where Drew is?" Jamie, looking very attractive in black tie, stared over Eve's head. "I bet he wanted to stop the ex from coming but she's involved with Morgan now. He never gets left out of anything."

"I don't know anyone here, do you?" Eve glanced around at the crowd of beautiful people. Most were standing in little groups, smiling and talking, obviously well known to each other. The Establishment. She had never been part of it.

"Actually, yes," Jamie answered carelessly, secure in his own monied background. "I freely admit connections got me my job, but I think I've proved myself."

"You have indeed." Eve patted his arm, very glad of his company.

A moment later an attractive young woman swept up,

grasping Jamie around the waist. "Hello there, James. I was hoping we would meet up."

Not looking particularly thrilled, Jamie made the introductions, which the young woman acknowledged sweetly before bearing him off "for just a moment." Jamie looked beseechingly over his shoulder. It was Eve he wanted to spend all his time with. She looked quite wonderful tonight.

Left alone, Eve moved gracefully through the lovely expansive room pausing before a large portrait of what had to be the late Lady Forsythe.

"My mother."

She knew a moment before he came behind her it was Drew. She would respond to his shadow.

"You have her eyes and the curve to her mouth," Eve said, without turning. "She was beautiful."

"And so much more." Drew looked with deep nostalgia at his mother's painted features. The artist, a famous one, had painted her at the height of her beauty when she was the same age as he was now. Thirty-five. He had never learned to live without her. His mother had been the real sustaining force in their lives. But like his father, he had finally accepted.

"Now let's look at you." He turned her to him, hands remaining momentarily on her shoulders, *absorbing* her, a flame at the centre of his dark eyes. "You steal all the light."

Drew. Drew. Drew.

"I didn't want to let you down." She was aware her voice shook.

"And those beautiful diamond earrings?" He pushed back a long silky strand of her hair the better to see them, his fingertips brushing the side of her face. "Now who bought you diamonds?"

"Would you accept one of my admirers?" She allowed her green eyes to meet his. God, how could any woman control her responses with a man like this?

"Tell me all about it," he invited. "Actually *don't*. I don't want to know."

"The truth is they belong to a good friend of mine," Eve relented. "A twenty-first birthday present from her parents. Lisa is very generous."

"She must be, and that's nice, but you must get some of your own."

"Not at the moment." She smiled, swallowed up by those dark eyes. She had made Ben give up one of his part-time jobs.

"Come and meet people." Drew took her by the arm—skin on skin.

"I'm a bit nervous," she admitted. A party as big as this attended by so many sophisticated, influential people would be a test.

"You'll learn to get over that very quickly," he promised. Sure of it instinctively. "Anyway, Evie—" his glance caressed her face "—it doesn't show."

Is everyone staring at me, Eve thought, or is it a figment of my imagination? It wasn't. But Drew was the cause of it. She was simply the mystery woman by his side. That's why the heads were turning. Who was she? What was she? It was odd they had never seen her before.

Drew appeared oblivious to it all. People smiled at his approach. He gave them his extraordinarily winning smile back. Where his father was viewed with a mixture of caution and envy, sometimes a well-hidden hostility, Drew could have campaigned for first president of the republic.

Soon she was shaking hands. Drew introduced her as

Miss Eve Copeland, a valued member of his team. Some names and faces stood out. The people who appeared often in the newspapers or the society sheets, others became a blur even though Eve was very good at sorting out names and faces. She couldn't help noticing Drew's ex-wife standing with a big man in a double-breasted dinner jacket. He had the look of a footballer but Eve knew that was Peter Morgan, the entrepreneur. Carol was trying not to look their way, her expression and the arrangement of her limbs full of considerable hauteur. She wore the kind of dress one saw in Paris Vogue, stunning but impossible to sit down in. Her long dark hair was pulled back and studded with jewelled stickpins. She looked very exclusive and she'll catch up with me some part of this evening, Eve thought. Carol Forsythe wasn't the sort of woman to let go.

It happened a short time before they were due to go into supper. Eve, who had been sitting talking to Elizabeth Garratt and one of Elizabeth Garratt's old friends, excused herself briefly to have a word with Jamie when Carol surprised her by grasping her by the arm.

"Ah, Miss Copeland, we meet again."

Eve turned full around smiling pleasantly. "Good evening, Mrs. Forsythe. How are you?"

"Never been better in my life." It was said so tightly it was almost a snap. "I must say you look very well." This accompanied by a top-to-toe inspection.

"Thank you. You look stunning yourself."

"Let's sit down for a moment, shall we?" Carol shifted her hand back to Eve's arm.

"Just for a moment I'm afraid." Eve allowed herself to be propelled into a quiet corner. "I'm keeping Mrs. Garratt company."

"Obviously you're one of those people who's always looking for opportunities."

"I guess so. They don't knock twice."

"You're a go-getter." Carol sought to label her. "I've made a few inquiries. It seems you've won your way into the corporation's good books in a very short time."

"That's good." Eve looked directly into the other woman's eyes. "I work hard and I enjoy what I'm doing."

"I'm sure." Carol gave a tight smile. "Most women would have given their eyeteeth to become Drew's assistant."

"Executive Assistant," Eve corrected mildly, determined not to rise to the bait. "He's a great boss to work for. Inspirational."

"And *eligible* now I've left him." Carol gave her a hard meaningful smile.

"That's where I'm different, Mrs. Forsythe." Eve directed a serious gaze. "I have a *career*."

"So did dear Susan," Carol Forsythe pointed out, suddenly looking furious at the thought. "Let me tell you about her."

Eve resolved to stop that at once. "I'd prefer you didn't. There's a theory talking about people is a sin."

Carol stared at her, then laughed. "Then most of us are going to hell. Susan married David for the title and the money. Everyone knows that. She's much more in love with Drew. But she'd never admit it even to herself."

"Under the circumstances, that might be very wise." Eve masked her own upset. "But none of it has anything to do with me."

"You're not stupid, are you?" Carol gave her a shockingly bitter look. "You don't *look* stupid. You forget Drew was my husband. I know these people backwards. I know, for instance, Drew is looking for an affair with you. If it hasn't already started. He's not a man to waste time.''

It crossed Eve's mind not for the first time, Carol was still in love with her ex-husband. "Your information, Mrs. Forsythe, is incorrect," she said, surprised by the calmness of her own voice. "You must excuse me. I told Mrs. Garratt I'd only be a few minutes.''

"Frightened of what you might hear?" Carol challenged.

"What *is* there to hear?" Eve stood up. "Everyone looks perfectly happy to me. Lady Forsythe has been glued to her husband's arm all night.''

"She's no fool," Carol said with hard irony. "Oh, she cares about David, I grant you, though I've always found him a touch daunting. Drew is the *only* one he loves, now the saintly Madelyn has gone. I have my suspicions Carol made her little play for Drew years ago, but he wouldn't have noticed anyone he was too busy trying to get over me. A bit of a paradox that. He didn't value me when he had me.''

"Broken marriages are always painful," Eve said, thinking Carol's comment contained more spite than truth.

"You do know he finds it impossible to remain faithful?" Carol, sitting stiffly on a Louis armchair, looked up.

"So do most men," Eve answered with visible tension.

"That sounds extraordinarily bitter." Carol stared at her. "So you *do* know?"

"I try to steer clear of involvements, Mrs. Forsythe. I had a very unhappy home life. I'm not about to make any mistakes.''

"Well, good for you." Relief translated into a big smile. "I would have stayed with Drew forever but I couldn't forgive his constant straying. It broke my heart."

The battleground of marriage, Eve thought, trying to deal with two conflicting sides of a story. Carol had sounded blisteringly bitter. Could it possibly be true, even during his short marriage Drew had strayed when it suited him? She was afraid to think of it. He had so disarmed her with his deep sincerity. Yet hadn't she formed her own opinion before she came to work at TCR? The strikingly handsome and sexy Drew Forsythe was always photographed with some beautiful young woman on his arm. On his own admission, it was he who had left the marriage allegedly because Carol had refused to bear him a child. He certainly wasn't deeply involved with anyone Eve knew of, at the moment. Except, quite extraordinarily, *her* and that involvement hadn't gone beyond her own set boundaries. To be alone with Drew was to surrender to a dangerous desire. She couldn't help that. She was human, not the smoothly running machine she had thought herself. Besides, she had learned the stark realities of life young.

Supper was superb. Set up in the high-ceilinged formal dining room which exuded a marvellous Anglo Raj atmosphere. The very long dark mahogany table had in fact been custom made in India surrounded by dark timbered elegant chairs upholstered in white as was the colour of the walls. Four brass candelabra in glass storm shades hung suspended from gleaming brass ropes over the table and a magnificent five-foot-high teak headboard, beautifully fretted and carved stood atop a teak and glass cabinet. The beautiful white flowers arranged in a pair of beautiful silver swans beguiled Eve's eye.

She adored flowers and always managed to bring a small bouquet home, but she had never seen such a lavish display. Flowers lit up every room from simple to breathtakingly bold. They must have cost a fortune, but then, the Forsythes were in the position to pay.

Her first view inside Drew's family home. She would have lots to tell Ben.

Drew, even over supper, worked the room, using his considerable charm on the obviously flattered guests. Or maybe he wasn't *using* it at all, Eve thought, observing him through her eyelashes. His manner, she had since come to know, was entirely natural. Even Sir David's frosty blue eyes softened whenever his son moved into orbit. Whoever else found Sir David Forsythe abrasive, he was a very different man with his son. Mercifully Drew had been able to live up to all his father's expectations, Eve thought. Another son, less brilliant, might have found it an entirely different story. Lost in her thoughts, Eve was a little startled when Jamie, who had hastened to rejoin her, touched her on the arm.

"You're not eating much. Try those little crab mille-feuilles or whatever they are called. They're simply out of this world. I don't know if we're supposed to eat the nasturtiums." He grinned.

"You can if you like." Eve smiled. "They're perfectly edible but I think they're supposed to be a decoration, and very pretty, too." Such variety of wonderful food had been assembled. Roast beef, pork, baked glazed hams, turkey, sides of smoked salmon, marvellous seafood, Gulf of Carpentaria prawns, crayfish, lobster, shellfish arranged in easily handled chunks inside the carapace. There was a hill of glistening caviar piled high on an iced silver tray, salads of all kinds, hot dishes brought out halfway through served with fragrant steaming rice.

Another sideboard held all the sweet delights. Tortes, gateaux, little latticed fruit pies, cheesecakes, profiteroles with pastry cream and toffee icing arranged in a pyramid, delectable confections for the chocolate lover....

I have to be the only one here who isn't hungry, Eve marvelled. Even the bone-thin Carol was busy forking succulent grey pearls of Iranian caviar, hideously expensive, into her mouth.

Towards the end of supper Sir David spoke about the project so dear to his heart, thanking Elizabeth Garratt for seeing the value inherent in it and graciously agreeing to selling them a crucial amount of land. He even mentioned Eve's part in the negotiations with a small smile of approval. Then he nodded to Drew who took over from his father, elaborating on project Capricornia for the benefit of guests.

''God, isn't he just so smooth and confident,'' Jamie whispered in Eve's ear admiringly. ''Just look at the way everyone has their body turned towards him. The way their faces light up. They weren't doing that when Sir David was talking.''

Eve had noticed that, as well.

After supper people began to stream out of the sets of French doors onto the broad verandas that surrounded the house on three sides. Moonlight showed up a beautiful garden, the air redolent with all the heady scents of summer.

''Now where are you going?'' a so attractive deep voice asked her.

Eve turned to face him. ''I should be thinking about going home.''

''Haven't you enjoyed yourself?'' Drew caught hold of her hand, steering her away from the crowd towards the library.

"I have," she said when Carol and her disclosures had thoroughly rattled her. "I'm entranced with the ancestral home. It's very splendid but it has a welcoming atmosphere. You must have had a happy childhood here."

"Not always," he said surprisingly. "Dad was really plugged in to the job of mining magnate. He was away a great deal. Even when he was home it wasn't always easy to see him. I know my mother was very lonely at times. Oh, she filled her life with friends and the charity work she held dear, she just didn't get much quality time from her husband. Dad wasn't an easy man. Still isn't."

"He adores you," Eve insisted.

"We've settled down." Drew shrugged. "Dad had to put up with a lot of rebellion in my early days. I wanted him to know I'm *me*. I just wish my mother could have survived. Dad is indestructible."

"Can anyone really say that?" Eve looked up at him remembering the untimely *undreamed* death of the Princess of Wales.

"I suppose not," he agreed. "The most I can say is, he's always seemed that way."

Eve nodded and walked ahead into the book-lined library, the parqueted floor covered with a magnificent Persian rug. "This is a wonderful room," she said, excitement beating at her senses.

"Even better." He smiled. "There's no one here. I can have you to myself for a few moments. How are you getting home?"

"With Jamie." She had to make herself secure.

"You know he's more than a little in love with you?" His voice was gentle and soft.

"It's not *serious*." Eve shook her head. "Jamie knows I don't mix business with pleasure."

"You did. Once upon a time." He perched on the end of a desk, marvellously handsome in his beautifully cut dinner clothes.

"You're much too attractive, Drew. But I have to resist flirting with danger." She exhaled a deep sigh.

"Flirting?" the mocking eyebrow shot up. "That's not the word for *you*."

"Maybe not." She picked up a leather-bound book on the circular table, then put it down. "My friend, Lisa, calls me a control freak."

"It must cost you dearly." He seemed to be devouring her with his eyes. "You're full of strong emotions. I sensed that the very first day in the lift, for all the chaste buttoned-up image."

"Damn, is that how I appeared." Eve started to turn away, thinking she couldn't take that dark gaze much longer.

"Well, God knows, you're chaste." His words were light, laconic, but she swung on him.

"And you want to change that?"

"I'm *going* to change it, Evie," he said, a faint almost undetectable iron determination in his face. "But only when you're ready. For now I have to content myself with sitting back and observing. What did Carol have to say to you, by the way?"

"She was striving to warn me against you." Eve settled into an armchair upholstered in ruby leather, fingering the carved arms.

"One has to be a bit wary of Carol. I suppose she divined my interest in you?"

"I gather I'm one of many."

He looked horrified. "Is that what she told you?"

Eve stared at the coffered ceiling before answering. "She said your marriage never stood a chance because you were unfaithful.'' Despite herself, her voice broke a little.

"She upset you." It wasn't a question but a flat statement.

"I don't like being caught in the middle."

"How could that be?" he answered swiftly. "Carol and I are divorced. I would have thought she had something serious going with Morgan. That's the word around town."

"And does it hurt?" Eve asked, intent on his expression.

He looked back steadily into her eyes. "What difference would it make if I told you? You seem to have made up your mind."

His anger targeted her now. "It's just because—" Some instinct made Eve hug herself tightly. "It's because…"

"You care?" he challenged her. "Or can't you live with that?" Then abruptly, "I'm sorry, Eve. Carol lied to you. It's over."

"I think it'll be better if I go home." Eve stood up, desperately penitent this element of hostility had crept in. "Thank you for a wonderful evening."

"You're welcome," he said, coming to his feet. The brilliance of her eyes matched the cobwebby shimmer of her beaded dress but her lovely skin had paled. She looked heartbreaking all of a sudden. He had a vivid mental picture of a little girl in a family deserted by husband and father. Pain had fashioned her. The pain of betrayal. He knew he was going to have to work hard to overcome it.

"Evie," he said tenderly, as she went to hurry past him, catching her into his arms, exquisitely conscious of her slender woman-scented body.

For an instant she yielded, not daring to take a breath against the sweet, sharp spear of desire.

"I want to be alone with you."

"It's not possible." Yet every day her feeling for him was getting harder to subdue.

"Yes, it is." He lowered his dark head, brushing his mouth against the smoothness of her cheek. "Come home with me."

"No." Ridiculous when she wanted him so desperately she could have dissolved in tears.

"I want to make love to you. Touch you all over with my mouth and hands. Trust me, Eve. Trust me. You *must*."

Still she shook her head, afraid of her increasing dependence on him. What was love, a kind of madness? *Love?* Wasn't it time she confronted her true feelings instead of treating it like a blazing affair?

"I can't, Drew," she uttered wretchedly, shadowed by her past.

"Listen to me, Evie." He turned her face up to him, beseeching when he never had in his life. "I never imagined…"

Such a wild yearning rocked her, her heart, her head, her insides. What was he doing to her, bonding her to him so she would never get away? Had she completely forgotten her mother's suffering? Because of what? This man's magic. His warm sweetness, his burning ardour.

"Let me tell Jamie I'm taking you home," he said with the sharp imperative of passion. What was happening was agony, when desire had its own way.

Susan, sweeping through the house, came upon them so soundlessly, Drew wheeled in surprise.

There was silence for a moment and Eve's stomach

contracted at the wounded look on Lady Forsythe's face. Even her skin turned transparent.

"Are we being missed?" Drew asked in his smooth tantalising voice.

"Yes." The answer was very faint, as though Susan was desperate for air.

"I must leave anyway." Eve found the strength to make the break. A desperate run for it, really. "Thank you for a wonderful evening, Lady Forsythe. I've so enjoyed being in your beautiful home." In all her life Eve had never felt such tension that now arose around all three of them.

"It was a pleasure to have you, Eve." Gallantly Lady Forsythe rallied, trying to fight back her own hopelessly mixed up feelings. "Why don't we have lunch sometime?"

"That would be lovely." Impossible to say anything else.

"Good night, Drew." Eve turned her face to him, seeing his handsome mouth twist.

"Whatever makes you happy." He shrugged.

"Your father wants to speak to you, Drew," Lady Forsythe said, making a huge effort to sound normal. "Something about the Poiynton takeover."

"It looks like we're back to shop talk," Drew said.

# CHAPTER SIX

WEEKS went by when Eve immersed herself in her work. Inexplicably Drew had drawn back, as confident and charming as ever but concentrating on what was very clearly a big job. Although they continued to work on project Capricornia together, there were other more pressing matters to occupy his mind, like the reopening of the Mount Maratta mine in the North West of the state. Eve arrived at work one Monday morning to be told Sir David and Mr. Forsythe had taken the company plane to the site of the old copper and gold mine along with their head geologist and didn't expect to be returning for possibly a week.

"Mr. Forsythe wants you to close that Santro deal, Eve," Sara Matheson told her. "I must say he has great confidence in you."

"I hope it's deserved." Couldn't he have told her he would be away? Eve thought, feeling a rush of acute disappointment. She had grown used to their close working relationship. Perhaps *too* used.

In her office she reached for the phone, setting up an appointment to meet with Richard Wilson at Pearce Musgrave. They ought to be grateful. She had put a lot of business their way. Now she had to let her work dominate her mind.

The phone woke her. Eve pulled herself out of her sleep, groping for the receiver. What time was it? Two-thirty.

Who would be ringing at this time? Ben, she thought with a deep sense of relief, was home and sound asleep.

"Eve Copeland," she said into the receiver, her voice husky with sleep.

"Jack, here," a familiar voice said. "I thought it best if this came from me, Eve. It will be on the news in the morning. Sir David suffered a massive heart attack sometime late this afternoon. They were out at the mine. Sadly, he was dead by the time help got to them."

Eve jumped out of bed in shock. "Jack, I'm so sorry. I didn't know Sir David well but I thought, like Drew, he was pretty well indestructible. He always looked so fit and well."

"I know." Jack's voice cracked.

"And Drew. How terrible!"

"He was totally unprepared." Jack's tone conveyed it had been a sad phone call. "He sounded broken up. He'll be bringing his father back today. God, Eve, it's going to be awful."

And awful it was.

The newspapers were full of it. Sir David, alive and talking on T.V. How does the family stand it? Eve thought. But shock had taken hold of them all. Even the business world and the wider community were stunned. Sir David, if he hadn't exactly been loved, had risen head and shoulders above his peers. A mining magnate of the old school and a legend in the state. What was worse, only for the remoteness of the mine's location, he might have been saved had paramedics with their equipment been on hand. A frantic Drew had performed cardiopulmonary resuscitation to no avail. Sir David's time had been up. There was a big photograph of Drew and Lady Forsythe in the front of Sunday morning's paper coming away from the funeral home. Both were dressed in black. Both looked strained and sombre.

"What a sad life it is," Ben remarked solemnly, looking over Eve's shoulder. "Drew is going to have an awful lot on his shoulders. He might have expected his father to last a good ten years at least. And what about Lady Forsythe? She's lost a husband. I expect he left her very well off, but her whole position has changed."

Ben squeezed Eve's shoulder then walked to the door to start the afternoon stint at McDonald's. "Drew contacted you yet?"

"Of course not." Eve shook her head. "There's far too much going on for him to think about me. He has a married sister in London. She'll be returning for the funeral. There must be a hundred and one things for him to think about and attend to."

"It's tough, I agree. But most people seem to think he's ready to step into his father's shoes."

Eve turned back the thoughts that sprang to mind. They were too deeply tangled. "What time do you think you'll be home?" She turned to search her brother's face. He was getting too thin, the result of too much work and too little relaxation.

"Simon has asked me over to his place later. He wants me to help him out with an assignment. Don't worry, he always feeds me first. Mrs. Bolton is a great cook."

Left alone, Eve decided to get out and go for a walk. It was a beautiful day outside, the worst of the summer heat was over and there were many parks in the area. She felt incredibly restless, incredibly sad, forced to accept, when it really came down to it, she was no one in Drew's life. She had not seen him now for more than a week. Surely it seemed longer? A kind of anguish stirred in her. Once you allowed strong emotion into your life you were never the same. It was painfully apparent Drew wasn't coming to see her. He didn't need her. He was caught back into his own world. She couldn't help but remember how Susan had reached up to stroke his face that very first day. It was meant to be affection but Eve had caught the fascination in her eyes. A woman's intuition. It was pretty well infallible.

Now the grief and terrible bleakness of loss. Eve felt pity.

She took her time walking around the park. Children were playing on swings and whooshing down the slippery slides, young mothers in attendance. As always there were lovers lying on the grass, heads resting against one another's, pointing with locked hands to the big beautiful kite that was moving in an arc across the sky.

What have I got myself into? Eve thought. She was very glad, then, there had been no sexual involvement. She had already arrived at a point where the attachment was too great. And what about her job? Sir David's death had changed everything. Drew would be called on to play an ever larger role. What a letdown it would be to work for someone else. But in the end, mightn't it be for the best? She had stepped out of line. Now she was on her own. Aloneness was home territory.

Home again at the apartment, she showered briskly, shampooed her hair, then dressed in fresh clothes, a white silk top and a favourite floral skirt that created a breeze when she moved. She hadn't heard a word from Lisa for two days. Perhaps she'd better give her a call. Everyone was trying to come to terms with Sir David's sudden death. And what would happen to that legendary wealth? The young widow would be left very comfortable, but Drew was the heir. His sister, Anne, would be amply provided for, though she had married very well from all accounts. Her husband's uncle was an earl.

Eve picked up a book and tried to read. It was dusk before she stirred, going to the window not quite sure if a car had pulled into their drive. If it had, it was a very smooth engine.

She flicked the vertical blind, her whole being injected with adrenalin when she saw it was Drew. He was standing outside his Jaguar, turning the key in the lock. Immediately she went to the door and held it open.

"Drew!"

He put his arms around her and she clung tightly, wordlessly offering up her deepest sympathy.

His abundant vitality was diminished, his handsome face full of strain.

"How are you?" She drew back and their eyes met. Locked, as though each was looking into the other's soul.

"How right you were, Evie." He shook his head sadly. "Do we *ever* know?"

Spontaneously she took his hand, leading him into the small living room. "Come in. Can I get you anything at all?"

"Maybe some tender loving care." The flashing smile was a mere shadow of itself. "I've missed you, Evie." It was said with a sudden injection of fierceness.

"I've missed you, too." She was full of anguish for him. "I haven't been able to get you out of mind. How is Susan?" she said with genuine pity.

"Devastated, as you can imagine. It'll take quite a while for reality to hit. Here, sit down beside me." He caught her back to him, the need in his eyes warming the blood in her veins. Then when he had her on the sofa, he leaned forward and buried his face in her breast.

"Evie."

She had never known anything so intimate. She who had felt herself abandoned by him. "I wanted to come before but you can't know what it's been like." He sounded deeply troubled. "Dad's affairs are *enormously* involved. It'll take months to work it all out. Maybe even years. Susan is distraught. I gather they had an argument of some sort, but she won't speak about it."

Eve felt a sudden pang of anxiety. "You have no idea?"

"Sometimes imagining is far worse than reality," he said in a sombre voice. "I only know Dad was far from relaxed. I sometimes thought he hardly heard a word I said."

"He might have been feeling ill." Eve felt frightened.

"God knows." His dark eyes were bleak. "Not enough to say anything. Andy Stewart, our geologist, felt it, too. Something was nagging at him. Now we'll never know."

"I'm so sorry, Drew."

"Just let me hold you," he said. "This isn't really happening, Evie, is it? It's a dream."

"Sudden death is like that." Eve's thoughts, as always, turned to her mother.

"*You're* all right?" Now he could see the extent of her own unhappiness.

"Of course, I was worried about you." She knew all about desolation and grief. Loss and agony.

"I really do love you, Evie," he said.

She went hot all over. "Hush!" She ran her finger across his mouth a little frantically as if to stop him. "You don't know what you're saying."

"I've never been more sure of anything in my life."
His voice that had carried signs of grief now sounded
strong and calm. "I think I must have fallen in love with
you the moment I saw you. Something about you held
me spellbound. Like a painting. Now I've got to know
you so well."

Despair and joy warred in her. "Drew, we've only
known one another such a very short time." She faltered
briefly. "I'm afraid of so much emotion."

"I know that." A deep protectiveness flared in him.
"I've tried to be as gentle with you as I know how.
You're a little in love with me, Evie."

"I am?" She tried to smile, her face very soft and
full of heart.

"Yes, you know you are. You've got shadows under
your lovely eyes. Don't they have something to do with
me?"

"They have *everything* to do with you," she admitted,
and suddenly kissed the hand that was caressing her
cheek. "I thought you weren't going to contact me at
all."

He looked at her in surprise. "You must know I
would."

"It doesn't matter now," Eve said huskily, and made
to move. She had to get him something to eat. Always
very lean, he had lost weight, the creases in his cheeks
more pronounced.

"Don't get up," he said in a slow deep voice that set
every nerve quivering. "It's very important to me to
have you beside me."

"I only wanted to get you something to eat."

"Darling Evie, I'm ravenous for you," he said, and
pulled her right into his arms. "You're so warm and
sweet, flowing with comfort. Sometimes I think I've

only loved two people absolutely *completely*. You and my mother. Does that sound terrible? With Dad gone and Anne and her husband away. Of course I love them, too. Hell, it's impossible to explain. Kiss me, Evie. Put me back together.''

Her green eyes filled with tears, showing the depths of her own emotional intensity.

"Evie." His hand encircled her nape. "There's nobody. Just nobody like you. You're a jewel. My jewel."

She moaned a little as he rocked her, placing her head very gently in the crook of his arm. Then he lowered his head with quickening desire, catching up her mouth with his own, feeling her beauty and tenderness flow all over him, this marvellous, mysterious girl.

"I'll never let you go," he muttered, his mouth moving across her face but always returning to her mouth. This was what he wanted. This was what he needed. His whole body throbbed. Such passion lay below her serene exterior. She was all excitement but in such a *natural* way, a combination of delicacy and a woman's unique power. It was true what he had said. He had been drawn to her on a glittering magnetic current. Now it was impossible to get away.

He held her so close he could feel her lifeblood pounding in her, matching the wild rush of his own. He couldn't imagine not having her, his hands finding the gentle contours of her breasts. There was such an elegance to her, a proportion, the long delicate bones, her fragile ankles and beautifully turned legs. Her full skirt had eased up and now he sought the satin curve of her hip, such hunger raging through him he thought he couldn't live with it.

"Where's Ben, Evie?" he asked urgently, betraying his intentions.

The air was so fraught, so impassioned, between them, he spoke in undertones.

She opened her eyes, a hint of panic in them. "He won't be home until late. Drew, we're going to have to stop now."

"I can't, Evie. I'm sorry. Don't ask me to. You belong to me." Then he questioned, "Could you fall pregnant?"

"Is that what you want?" She was on the edge of total surrender even when she tried to hide it.

"Our child would fill me with wonderment," he said in a voice full of emotion, "but I don't want to do a thing wrong. I want to marry you, Evie. I want to glory in you on our wedding day. I want to carry the sight of you as a bride through all the days of my life. I want our first child to arrive in good time. But right now I need you so badly, I can almost feel to *hell* with everything! Except I couldn't bear to hurt you."

An incredible new world billowed up before her. Drew's wife? Her shock and the avalanche of emotion was too great to be contained. Marriage was a tremendous thing. A frightening thing. It could lead to heaven. Or hell. "I can't marry you," she said when her emotions were soaring.

"You don't think I'm going to settle for mistress?" He spoke with the first sign of humour.

"Drew, you're mad."

"Yes, I am," he agreed. "Mad for you. Will you let me make love to you?"

There was no other answer she could give. "Yes," she whispered while the world tilted. If I have nothing else, she thought, I'll have this to remember for the rest of my life.

He carried her through to her bedroom, laying her on

the bed, his hands gentling her, honeying her with their exquisite strength, sliding off her clothes in this quite ordinary room that now seemed beautiful, unfamiliar, suffused with gold and amber.

"Let me look at you." He bent over her, so young and vulnerable, his dark eyes brilliant with the pleasure the sight of her gave him. Then he began kissing her, slow exploratory kisses all over her body, while enraptured little sounds sighed out of her. So this was what it was like to be caught up in a great passion. It was worth all the pain.

He was the consummate lover. Even with no experience at all Eve couldn't fail to grasp that. He was bringing her, oh, so slowly to the extremes of yearning, protracting the ecstasy, until she was helplessly calling his name. Then he turned her, locked her to his own now naked body, passion burning stronger than any grief.

"For the first time, Eve," he whispered, finding her innocence enchanting.

"The first time," she said, locking away the powerful sight of him inside her head.

"You're the only woman I love," he said with intense feeling. "Everything's fine. I'll go very slowly." He stroked her breast while feverishly she opened her mouth to his kiss. There was nothing and no one to hold on to. But Drew.

It was perfect. Dazzling joy. Above all. It was love.

Everything changed after that, though Eve did her level best to remain in the background, fairly sure no one inside the corporation knew of their involvement. She was adept at hiding her feelings. As was Drew, she observed. But then everyone was subdued, Sir David's state funeral still very much in everyone's mind.

Such a brief space of time for so much to have changed, Eve thought. She was torn between wonderment and the scary feeling life was speeding out of her control. Drew being Drew was so very sure of himself. But she was faced with a whole lot of unresolved feelings. She had even begun to *look* like a different person as though the overwhelming excitement of their sex life, for Drew wanted her to be with him often, showed in her manner, her speech and the hectic blossoming of her looks. Her abundant hair glowed, so did her eyes and her skin. She looked like she had been made over inside and out.

"You're in love with him, aren't you?" Ben asked over supper.

"I suppose it shows."

"Heck, yes," Ben exclaimed. "The fellow who said love puts a bloom on a woman was right."

"Charm, I think it was," Eve corrected. "Charm puts a bloom on a woman. I'm sure it was J. M. Barrie."

"As in 'Peter Pan'? I'm crazy about Julia Roberts." Ben made the leap to the movie, based on the book, where the enchanting actress played Tinkerbell.

"He's asked me to marry him," Eve now confided, thinking it was high time to let her brother know. She kept so much boxed up inside herself. And this was something so profoundly life changing.

"Good God!" Ben's hazel eyes leapt to hers. "When was this?"

"A few weeks ago."

"And you've been holding out on me?"

"I can't seem to get it straight in my mind." Eve stretched out an apologetic hand. "You know what I'm like."

"Hell, Evie, I think you'll have to do something about it." Ben frowned. "Drew Forsythe is talking marriage?"

"That's what I said." Eve bit her full bottom lip, still not believing it.

"Wow! I knew you were getting together but I didn't know you were that close."

"Probably his father's death precipitated it," Eve said, her stomach churning with unspecified anxieties. As was to be expected, the bereft Lady Forsythe was leaning on Drew for support. Even Carol Forsythe seemed to be always on hand to offer Drew sympathy.

"So what's the big problem?" Ben asked. "Surely you're not worrying about me?"

"Of course I worry about you," Eve said.

Ben watched her with concern. "Nothing will separate us, Evie, but I don't expect you to defer your happiness because of me. Besides, I'll have Lisa to comfort me." He grinned.

"You're just friends."

"You're kidding." Ben barked out a laugh. "We've moved beyond that, Evie. I'm a red-blooded male."

"Don't let a love affair complicate your life," she warned.

"What if I said Lisa is happy to wait?" Ben watched her.

"I'd better have a talk to Lisa," Eve said with a mixture of concern and humour.

"Have you told her about Drew?"

"The first and only person I've told is *you*," Eve admitted.

"That's fine. But why do you look threatened?" Ben knew his sister so well.

"I don't mean to sound a coward but I'm a little frightened of what's happening to me, Ben. Drew is so *positive* I don't think I have the strength to withstand him.''

"I can understand that. It's very easy to visualise. He's such a dynamo. I could hit it off with Drew as a brother-in-law, no trouble.''

"He's been married before,'' Eve said, haunted by the fact. "And Carol is still circling.''

"Maybe, but that's not the point. They couldn't hit it off. They're *divorced*. Surely you can accept that?''

"If I'm honest I'd say acceptance isn't one of my strengths. I'm in love with him, Ben, but I have to face the fact I don't know him that well.''

"You're just making excuses," Ben said, almost sadly. "What's really worrying you, Evie? Something is locked away there.''

She hesitated, but only for a moment, desperately wanting to unburden herself. "Never mention it, Ben," she said, "but I think his stepmother is in love with him, as well.''

Ben ran an agitated hand through his hair so it stood up wildly. "Get away with you. I thought all that was straightened out.''

"No, I think I was always right.''

"Maybe it's just a fantasy," Ben suggested. "Like women fall in love with their doctors. He's being very supportive at this time. You have a tender heart, Evie, you know how she must feel.''

"Absolutely.'' Eve sighed deeply but not without irony. "Maybe my being in love with Drew is a perfect fantasy, as well.''

# CHAPTER SEVEN

Short months after Sir David's death, construction had started on the small exclusive resort that was to fund the research centre. The centre itself was finally through the red tape but work would not commence until the following year by which time the resort would be nearing completion. There would be no Sir David to preside at the unveiling. The project that had meant so much to him would be brought to completion by his son.

Eve still remained as David's executive assistant, but there were many departments involved in the project: legal, public relations, a team from finance and the environment, architects, engineers, all doing their utmost to ensure the project would come in on time and stand as a fitting memorial. It was so very work-intensive, Eve was torn between an acute disappointment and a kind of relief she and Drew never had a moment alone. She herself was kept busy on the developmental program liaising with all the other groups.

"I think it's high time you had a break." Drew appraised her pale face after a late-night meeting. "I want to take a look at what's happening at the resort. It would be good to have a day or two to ourselves. Pack a bag for tomorrow morning. We'll go up in the company jet. You might schedule that for ten sharp, okay?" he said as he came to his feet, starting to rebutton his shirt at the neck and adjusting his tie.

"No problem." Tired as she was, Eve found it difficult not to jump for joy. Long months of concentration had gone into all the planning. It would be wonderful to simply sit back and relax with Drew at her side.

It didn't work out like that. When Drew arrived in the office after an early morning appointment with the banks, he was accompanied by Lady Forsythe wearing a beautiful resort-style pants suit, exactly the same colour as her eyes.

"Drew, have you got a minute?" his secretary begged almost frantically. "There are papers to be signed before you go."

Drew frowned and pulled away while Susan continued on to where Eve was standing. "Hello there, Eve." She greeted Eve with a friendly smile. "It looks like we're going to be companions for a few days."

Eve felt her heart sink. Still, she managed to sound pleasant. "You're coming to the resort, Lady Forsythe?"

"I *pleaded* with Drew to let me come," Susan confided. "I can think of no better way to honour David more than by this project. He discussed it with me so often. Of course I have a professional interest, as well. Public relations was my area. And please, call me Susan."

Eve made a little sound as though she recognised the honour. "Thank you, I'll be happy to, Susan."

"Drew isn't heeding my advice," Susan suddenly said, implying concern. "He has to slow down."

"There's a tremendous amount of work in his job." Eve wanted to say he was a dynamo.

"And I know he's very glad of all your assistance."

Eve was relegated to second secretary. "We're a team. Actually all of us have been working pretty well day and night to ensure the project comes in on time."

"And I'm thrilled," Susan said in a delighted voice. "Drew has already asked me to open it."

Eve was surprised how dismayed she felt. But *why?* Susan was Sir David's widow. It was a time-honoured gesture. Maybe she wondered why Drew hadn't told her. For that matter, when had Drew told Susan he was flying north? He'd only told her the night before. Obviously they were more intimate than Drew admitted. It occurred to Eve as she tried to swallow on the knot in her throat, she wanted to back out of this trip now that Susan was going. Susan's presence would ensure far less freedom and require a lot of polite conversation. Though she liked Susan for always being so friendly, she and Lady Forsythe led very different lives.

"I couldn't help that," Drew told Eve in a murmured aside as they were about to board the company jet.

"It's only natural Susan wants to see it," Eve said, her face smooth and calm. She knew what it was doing to her. No one else needed to know. Not even Drew.

Inside the aircraft they all snapped on seat belts embossed with the TCR logo. The jet was cleared for take-off and began taxiing down the runway rapidly gathering speed. Whatever Susan's private feelings regarding the exact relationship between Drew and Eve, her manner, pleasant though it was, clearly implied she had a higher place in the scheme of things. She was Lady Forsythe, Sir David's widow, and *family.*

As the aircraft lifted into the air Susan, seated on the leather banquette in the aft cabin, pulled a charming little face and lightly touched Drew's shoulder as though he *must* know she had a few little qualms about flying.

Eve, in her own comfortable padded armchair bolted like everything else to the floor, pulled out a report she was working on, resting it on the removable tray. They could have a private conversation if they wished.

Hours later when they arrived at the domestic terminal where they were met by a company employee, Eve felt she knew every nuance of Susan's soft melodious voice. Eve had to admire her, as well. Susan knew her stuff. Obviously she *had* listened when Sir David had talked about his pet project and kept abreast of things. She knew everyone's role and asked very intelligent questions, a lot of which Drew allowed Eve to answer.

In a way he's showing me off, Eve thought. Which meant he had to be proud of her. It was a good feeling.

"If I ever need another briefing session I'll know who to call on," Susan laughed, studying Eve with fresh eyes. She saw a young woman, coolly beautiful, with quite a brain and being given full rein to use it.

"Eve's very important to me," Drew said. "She makes things happen. She's won the respect of the rest of the team, as well. No mean feat when so much is expected."

"Vice-president material in time." Susan smiled. "I sometimes regret I gave up a very successful career."

They spent a couple of hours in the afternoon walking around the site holding in-depth conversations with the chief supervisor and key personnel. It was winter, or what passed for winter in Brisbane, the state capital, but over a thousand miles north the weather was glorious. The monsoonal season was over and the tourists had arrived in droves, seeking out all the wonders of the Great Barrier Reef. This was the time of year tropical North Queensland was invaded by southerners on holiday, turning normally sleepy coastal towns into playgrounds; relaxing on the beautiful beaches, filling the waterfront hotels and motels, enjoying seafood lunches and dinners in the restaurants that were dotted all over the beautiful coastline.

Susan was wearing a sunshine-yellow silk shirt and matching narrow-legged pants that afternoon, taking Drew's hand as he helped her across a planked area.

"So David's dream is really coming true," she said softly, tears gathering in her lovely blue eyes. "Oh, Drew, he was proud of you."

If Eve didn't feel abandoned she certainly thought Susan would have been happier had she stayed at home.

Later, the two women swam in the large free-form swimming pool at their hotel, while Drew attended to faxes and phone calls. Susan was looking almost fragile in a navy blue Lycra bikini. She had noticeably lost weight in the months since she had lost her husband. No swimmer, she cooled off quickly in the turquoise water then towelled herself off beneath the canopy of palms and tree ferns, wrapping her dark head in a yellow and navy Gucci scarf. Next she spread herself out on her brilliantly patterned towel, smiling and waving at Eve who was still lapping the pool.

It was all a daze, Eve thought, flooded with impressions of Susan and Drew together. *Dangerous relations,* she thought. Susan wasn't bothering to hide her affection.

Just as she was thinking of getting out, Eve saw Drew walking down through the terraced gardens. He was wearing a bright resort shirt over his swimmers, a fringed beach towel over his shoulder, his dark eyes shaded by a pair of Raybans. He looked wonderful, long tanned legs beautifully straight, his shirt hanging loosely over his taut, bronze torso. Susan must have thought he

looked wonderful, too, because as he stopped to say
something to her, she caught at his hand. She loves
touching him, Eve thought. In fact she can't keep her
hands off him. That had been apparent for most of the
day.

I have to trust him. Eve tried to fight out of her deeply
embedded scepticism. If I love him, even if I've had the
sense not to say it, *I have to* trust him. Drew was a
stunningly attractive man. Not only that, he had power
and a fortune. He was *exactly* what every woman
wanted. It would be very easy for the woman in his life
to become phobic. Hadn't Carol confided her endless
fears he was being unfaithful? It didn't help either
women had a habit of throwing themselves at him.

Whatever the exchange, it was brief. Drew threw off
his shirt and towel, walked round to the deep end of the
pool, to the delight of every woman in the vicinity, and
dived in. He surfaced beside Eve, putting up his hands
to slick back his dark hair. Wet, it clung to his beautifully shaped skull, beads of water sheening his smooth
tanned skin and the eyelashes a woman would die for.

"Hell," he said in exasperation. "It's hard to get you
alone."

Magnet-like, Eve stayed close to him. "Having Susan
along might explain a lot."

"Are you saying you're jealous?" It was impossible
to know if he was serious or teasing.

"No." She shook her gold head slowly. "I'm simply
stating a fact." Then, abruptly changing the subject,
"Would you like to race me?"

"Evie, you're good, but I'd win."

"Of course. You would have to give me a start."

"If I say yes, I want a promise out of you," he said,

dark eyes dancing. He was more handsome, more seductive, than any man had the right to be.

"I want to know what you're asking first," she said, feeling, extraordinarily, he had leaned forward and kissed her.

"I want you, Evie." His hands below the water held her tight around her velvet hips.

Every muscle tightened deep within her. The magic of being with him! But she was far too aware of Susan's presence and watching eyes.

"What if I say you have to live with it?" That when her whole body was avid for his.

"Is that so?" In a flash he ducked her, the two of them sinking beneath the water, his hands moving to cup her breasts cocooned in a white flower-strewn bikini top.

She was burning hot inside before he released her. "Drew, cut it out," Eve pleaded.

"Say please." He encircled her with his arms. "I'm tired of this, Evie. I never was good at playing games."

Her back to her, Eve wondered if Susan had left. "That from a top athlete," she jeered. "I've heard all about your track and field exploits at university. That's before you became the famous yachtsman."

"Susan's worrying you, is that it?"

Eve turned her body in the water. Susan was still there. Sitting up, dark glasses covering her eyes. "Only up to a point. But I wouldn't put it past her to come knocking on my door just to check where I was."

He shrugged a wide shoulder. "You'd be with *me*. Now let's drop the subject of Susan for a moment and have that race. Freestyle, I take it?"

"Backstroke," Eve announced. It was her best stroke. "But I want half the pool start," she warned.

"Take as much as you like." His smile was like a flash of light. "I'll still win." Which he did.

Dinner saw them all back together again. Susan must have searched her huge wardrobe for just the right clothes. Widow's weeds were out. She was wearing a long, one-shouldered jersey dress in broad black, white and sapphire stripes. Perfume rose from her clothes and she had tucked a fuchsia hibiscus behind her ear. So hard to fathom the human condition! Eve hadn't the slightest doubt Susan had cared deeply for her husband, a combination of respect and admiration, but she really was in love with Drew. It gave Eve no joy.

"I'm so pleased you've given me the opportunity to see over the construction, Drew," Susan said in her soft voice. "I can't wait for the research centre to take shape. This is the very nicest, most peaceful time I've had since…since…" She broke off with a little wince of distress.

"We're glad, Susan," Drew told her gently.

Their meal, when it came, was delicious. They lingered over coffee. All three went for an after-dinner stroll along the beach-front promenade, enjoying the brilliantly glowing stars and the breeze off the sea. Ménage à trois, Eve thought, herself excluded somewhat as Susan threw constant casual references to people and places Eve scarcely knew of into the conversation. For God's sake, why didn't I stay home? Eve thought.

"I think I'll go to bed now," Susan announced with a little yawn when they returned to the spacious foyer with its wonderful assemblage of orchids. "Early start in the morning."

Drew had suggested, to make her stay more pleasant they take the helicopter to Royal Hayman on the Barrier

Reef, have lunch there before returning late afternoon. The helicopter flight alone was a wonderful experience.

"Coming, Eve?" Susan asked, pairing them off. Two girls together. Female solidarity.

Drew answered her question, a glimmer of something Eve couldn't read in his eyes. "You go ahead, Susan, I want to fill Eve in on a few developments. She won't find it all out from the faxes."

"Oh." Susan shut off her disappointment before it showed on her face. "See you tomorrow then."

"Let's have a nightcap," Drew suggested a few moments after Susan had disappeared, taking Eve by the arm and steering her towards the lounge. "What will it be?"

"Just plain mineral water," Eve said, wanting a clear head.

"I should have guessed." He sounded amused.

When he returned, he found her poised like a creature about to take flight. "Running away, Evie?" There was a devastating tilt to his eyebrow.

"I don't want to sully your reputation."

He laughed deep in his throat. "Believe me, it's a lot better than you've ever given me credit for."

"You should strive to be perfect." Eve dipped her head, one side of her hair sliding across her cheek. "I'm sorry, Drew. You're too gorgeous and I'm a very suspicious woman."

"I was hoping I could help you with that." He put his hand over hers, feeling her whole body respond.

A deep silence, an intense communication. "So what's happening I should know about?" Eve finally managed.

He took a mouthful of his Scotch on the rocks. "Keep calm. You know it all. That was for Susan's benefit."

"Aren't you wicked," she mocked.

"I'm dying to be if you'd only give me half a chance." His eyes slid over her luminous beauty. She was wearing another one of her little slip dresses, sleeveless, a deep V-neck, the fluid rose-pink material sliding with such sensuousness over her body. He had never known a woman who so effortlessly combined a look of purity and unmistakable sexiness.

"Why do you look at me like that?" Eve asked, her eyes blazing emerald in the light from the wall bracket.

"Because you give me such pleasure," he answered simply. "Sometimes I think we're almost there but you slip away from me again. There are so many things I want to discuss with you but there never seems to be the time. Tell me about your father."

He almost saw the shutters come down.

"He lives while my mother died."

"Evie!" The note in his voice somewhere between sympathy and gentle censure made her flush.

"So I sound terrible. I don't want to talk about it, Drew." She raised a hand protectively to her throat.

"We discussed my father at length," he pointed out in a quiet reasonable voice.

So they had in the aftermath of their lovemaking.

"He was unfaithful to my mother." Evie tried again. "He betrayed us."

"Yet you speak of him with such feeling."

"I loved him once. I thought we were very close but he pushed me away. He rejected my mother. He punished us all."

"Do you ever see him?" Drew asked, his dark eyes intent on her changing expressions.

Eve gave a long sigh. "Drew, it does no good to talk about this."

*"Tell me."*

"He wants to come back into our lives. I don't know why."

"He's remarried, of course?"

"A woman young enough to be my sister. They have two children, a boy and a girl."

"Have you ever met them?"

"To what purpose?" Eve's expression froze.

"It might make a difference, Evie. They're your blood, are they not?"

"They're their mother's children," Eve pointed out bleakly. "Just as we are our mother's children. I'm not terribly good at forgiveness."

He could clearly see the embattled child. "That's because you were very badly hurt and at such a sensitive age. How does Ben feel about all this?"

"It's hot in here, isn't it?" Eve asked suddenly, looking around her for a path of escape.

"No."

"Ben thinks the same as I do," she spoke rapidly. "My father chose another life. He chose another family. End of story."

"All right." Drew broke off the interrogation as her agitation intensified. "Finish your drink. If you want to weep, I want it to be in my arms."

She shook her head. "Drew, *listen* to me."

"What is it?" He answered a little roughly wanting to sweep her up, lock his arms around her, draw her head against his chest.

She couldn't catch her breath. He seemed to look into her soul. "Since I met you I've gone a little crazy." This with a soft burst of broken laughter.

"What else is falling madly in love?"

"There's no way to know it will *last*." Even saying it was a knife in her breast.

"I hear your fears, Eve," he responded deliberately. "You want my advice? Concentrate on your own life."

The blood rose to her cheeks and she started to rise. "I'm going to bed."

He caught her hand. "So let's go. I'm done with waiting." He could feel her trembling as his grip tightened.

"I'm not a possession." She could feel the heat inside her increasing.

"Of course you aren't, and I've never treated you like one. I don't want to hear that again. You hunger for me, Eve, like I hunger for you. We only have to touch each other to discover that. Come on," he urged very gently, his arm enfolding her. "I'm going to undress you and kiss every inch of you better."

Upstairs in her hotel suite Susan lay wide awake, one hand cupping the other, right thumb rotating in her left palm, a form of acupressure she sometimes found worked for her when her mind started to whirl and she couldn't sleep. It wasn't working for her tonight. She had discarded the badly needed sleeping pills her doctor had prescribed for her in the early days after David's death.

Why had she come here? She writhed in shame. She was only jeopardising her dignity. When Drew had rung to say he could be out of town for a few days—she had done her utmost to pinpoint where—she had all but invited herself along on the trip. Now it was causing her acute embarrassment. Nothing was working out as she hoped.

Something was definitely going on between Drew and Eve Copeland. But how serious? Over the years Drew had had quite a few relationships, not the least of them marrying the glamorous, bone-selfish Carol. This girl was something else again. She was beautiful, clever enough to make herself a key player in project Capricornia, she was also very sensitive. Susan had seen flashes of understanding in her eyes as though in divining Susan's secret she somehow felt sorry for her. That in itself was a humiliation. Susan wasn't used to other women feeling sorry for her. Becoming Lady Forsythe had precipitated her into a world of power and envy.

Why, then, hadn't she taken more care? She made an attempt at self-justification. Because it had been impossible to predict what would happen? When *exactly* had her fond feelings for Drew tipped into infatuation? She decided she wasn't sure. Was it when she had lost the child? David had been away and Drew had been so kind and supportive. In the old days of chivalry he would have been a knight.

When had David begun to suspect her feelings for Drew had changed? She remembered him that night after the Capricornia party. The way he had turned and looked at her as if he had loathed what he understood. But he had never said anything, as though the shock was too great. A few short weeks were to elapse before his fatal heart attack. Was it the stress of knowing his wife had fallen in love with his own son? Susan twisted her hands until her knuckles gleamed white. To make everything so much worse they had quarrelled that last night. She had been frightened he was going to bring up the subject of Drew, but Drew was never mentioned. David *knew* beyond a shadow of a doubt his son was blameless. Falling in love had been solely Susan's mistake. It wasn't even *private*. If he had seen the light in his wife's eyes, so could others. It could become a public humiliation.

Then David had died.

It's impossible. Perfectly impossible, Susan thought, while deep inside her, wild hopes continued to flourish.

A woman on the brink.

# CHAPTER EIGHT

IT WAS Ben, in the end, who brought Eve's relationship with Drew to a sort of crisis point.

Taking an urgent phone call one afternoon—the meeting wasn't to be interrupted—Eve's face drained of all colour.

Drew who had swivelled in his chair to answer a staffer's question, turned back to scan her face.

"Evie, what is it?" He noticed that her hand was trembling and covered it with his own. "What's happened? You've gone as white as a sheet."

"It's Ben." She was speaking with great difficulty. "That was the Wesley Hospital. He's been admitted for observation. He collapsed during a lecture."

"Right." Drew stood up immediately, looking around the conference room. "That will do for this afternoon, people. Jamie, get all those documents signed for the Pacific Rim merger. I want them on my desk first thing in the morning. Lew, have your paperwork ready, as well." He put out his arm to Eve, shepherding her in. "Come, I'll drive you."

Eve thanked him, anxiety in her eyes. "I wish... I just wish he didn't work so hard. I've told him."

"He's young, healthy. But I agree he can't go on like this." Drew tightened his hand on her.

It was good to have Drew with her. It made Eve realise Drew made her feel safe.

When they reached the hospital Drew made enquiries

at reception, where they were directed to the ward where Ben had been taken.

They found him, sitting up in bed watching the television.

When he saw them his whole face lit up. ''Eve, Drew. Hi there!''

Eve went to him and gave him a tight hug. ''Ben, what happened?'' she said quietly.

There was the movement of chairs as Drew brought them up beside the bed.

''God knows!'' Ben shrugged. ''I even scared myself. One moment I was taking notes, feeling a little strange, the guy beside me called my name, then I must have collapsed. I don't even remember much about getting to the hospital. I'm fine now.''

''You stay there, Eve, I'll go talk to someone.'' Drew started to move off. ''Sounds like you've been overdoing it, Ben.''

''Hell, I'm not doing much more than Evie,'' Ben protested.

''That's not true, Ben.'' Eve slipped her hand over his on the covers. ''I've never known anyone who studies as long and hard as you.''

''I love it, Evie,'' Ben said. ''One day you're going to be very proud of me.''

''I'm proud of you now,'' she told him gently.

Drew, at the entrance of the ward, stared back. Both faces were in profile and he noted again the strong resemblance between sister and brother. Both had suffered when their mother had been so cruelly taken from them. Eve had tried to take the role of surrogate mother into her own hands. It, too, was draining her strength.

Out in the corridor he could see a tall middle-aged

man in a doctor's long white coat standing at the counter, in conversation with the nurse behind the desk. Drew approached, then when the man turned, asked if it was possible to speak to the doctor treating Ben Copeland. The tall man offered a hand. "Drew Forsythe, isn't it? I've seen you so many times in the paper I feel I know you. How may I help you? I'm looking after Ben. John Devon."

Drew smiled and shook hands while the nurse at the workstation looked on almost fondly. "I'd be grateful if you could let me know Ben's exact condition. I'm with his sister, Eve. She's talking to Ben now."

There was no hesitation. The doctor told Drew all he wanted to know. Ben had clearly been overdoing things. Hardly surprising when he was studying so hard. Dazzling promise from all accounts. It would make a difference if he could give up his night job and work only at the weekends. He wasn't eating regular meals and he wasn't getting enough sleep. There was nothing of any real concern. He was healthy enough but his body had simply said enough to all the stress.

Eve was quiet in the car going home. Drew wondered what anxieties were going on within her golden head. From all he had learned, Eve had been put under enormous pressure from her early adolescence. The past and the present were inextricably intertwined. Eve's life since her parents' divorce had been one of intensive commitment. She was unwavering in her devotion to her brother, indeed it worked both ways. He had observed the deep bond between the two of them, but it was obvious they needed help before Ben was ready to make his own way in the world. Certainly he deserved every encouragement to fulfil his ambitions. Medicine remained a noble profession. Maybe it was time to take both of them under his wing.

"No sense in coming back to the office." Drew drove her back to her apartment. "I still have a few things to clear up. What about dinner? We can pop in and see Ben again on the way. Or would you rather come over to my place. I can have everything we want sent in."

Eve couldn't curb the erotic rush. "You realise, don't you, we're going to end up in bed?"

He laughed softly under his breath, leaned down and kissed her on her full heart-shaped mouth, loving it when the tip of her tongue met his. "It's not just your body I'm after." He looked directly into her eyes.

"What else, Drew?" She stared back at him, so handsome, so vibrant, smiling at her. "I really want to know."

"Heck, you'll need a pen and paper to take notes," he teased. "Let's see. You have a first-class mind. I love the way we understand one another without talking. I love the way we enjoy the same things. I love your voice and the look in your green eyes. I admire the way you handle yourself and your life. I admire your devotion to Ben. I love the tender heart you tried so hard to hide. I love listening to you talk. So what do you see in me, Evie?" His eyes in the brilliant sunlight sparkled like jets.

"You're a magician," she said very seriously, "and I'm afraid of your power."

Ben looked better in the evening than he had that afternoon, but the look of exhaustion was plain in the shadows beneath his clear hazel eyes and the look of the boy behind the emerging man. But, as usual, he was bright and cheerful.

"Where are you off to after?" he asked, curling a long arm behind his head and studying the two of them with a warm, slightly teasing expression. It was very clear to Ben an enormous attraction existed between them. Eve, whether she admitted it or not, had been walking on air for months.

"Dinner." Drew gave Ben one of his flashing white smiles, dark eyes dancing. Hell, what more does he need? Ben thought wryly, in turn feeding on the older man's vitality. Drew was every inch a man's man but Ben could see quite plainly such was the sum of his assets he would bowl most women over. Pity the step-mother Eve had told him about was smitten.

"So enjoy yourselves." Ben gave them his blessing. "You'll look after my sister carefully, won't you, Drew?" Ben's eyes rested with unabashed love on his sister's face.

"With my life," Drew answered in such a deep, serious voice Eve, startled, blinked back tears.

"What more does she need?" Ben answered, well satisfied. "Off you go now. I'll be out of here tomorrow."

"And we might talk about a little break of some sort," Drew said. "I have the beach house at Noosa. You could take your books along. You might like to share with a friend. Take some time off, go surfing, enjoy the restaurants. We'll talk about it when I pick you up tomorrow."

Ben's handsome face reddened. "Gee, Drew. I don't know. I have a part-time job, lectures."

"You can catch up on them," Drew told him, seeming all of a sudden like an older brother. "Any part-time job will have to go on hold. It's absolutely essential you get back to your full strength."

Ben couldn't fail to read the message. It was a little

unsettling, Drew being so generous. He and Evie had always paid their own way, but it was obvious Drew meant to help. Could he accept? Ben felt with a flush of pleasure it would be wonderful to have a week off at the beach, catching the waves. Maybe Simon could come along with him? Lord knows the two of them spent overtime hitting the books.

It took only ten minutes more for them to reach Drew's penthouse apartment that had a marvellous view of the river and the city skyline. Eve had visited the apartment many times but each time she entered it was to a feeling of delight. Decorators working to Drew's brief had reworked a spacious but fairly plain area creating architectural details in the contemporary manner that gave the apartment great definition. The artworks were marvellous, the large-scale pieces of furniture, the few wonderful antiques for drama, the sense of intimacy within the large expanse. Nothing was delicate or dainty. The concept was bold, very masculine, the striking fabric that swathed several of the armchairs and sofas complementing the corded creamy beige of the upholstery in other seating areas. Robust ewers held lush indoor plants and the dining area set at the end of the large living room had hosted any number of formal, eighteen people, black-tie, sit-down dinners.

Tonight the circular stone table facing the view had been set for an occasion rather than a simple dinner for two. A fluted silver vase held a small posy of crimson rosebuds, an heirloom silver candelabrum holding slender dark green tapers stood at one end. The table was covered in a very beautiful white embroidered cloth, matching napkins looped with ivy, pure white, gold-rimmed bone china, gleaming silver flatware, crystal glasses. Drew always did like a bit of theatre, she thought smilingly. Still their sitting down together had never looked more ceremonial. There were sounds of activity coming from the galley kitchen completely screened off from the living room and Drew turned quickly to Eve.

"I've had someone from Margo's come in to fix dinner. They'll leave when it's all ready and we can serve ourselves."

Eve liked the idea. While Drew conferred with the chef, she walked out onto the terrace admiring the sparkling night-time view and the shining sweep of a city bridge across the broad stretch of water.

A few minutes later, having escorted their caterer to the door, Drew came out onto the terrace carrying two glasses of champagne. She could see the bottle reposing in a silver bucket on the table. Dom Pérignon.

"Are we celebrating something?" she asked, revealing her surprise at the very special "atmosphere."

"Who knows what can happen?" he gently mocked.

Drew wouldn't let her do anything, going back and forth to the kitchen bringing an entree of slow-roasted Tasmania salmon with a carefully composed salad that was as beautiful to look at as to eat, followed by breasts of chicken stuffed with lobster and basil, all served with little crispy rounds of freshly baked herb bread that melted in the mouth, with a light finish of beautiful fruit salad in lime and ginger syrup with Margo's coconut ice cream.

"I was hungrier than I thought." Eve gave a little blissful sigh, putting down her dessert spoon. "Thank you, Drew. I've never been so looked after in my life."

He looked up with searching dark eyes. "How do you know I didn't take aim for you that first day in the lift?"

"Aim, as in Cupid?" she asked.

"I made sure I interviewed you, didn't I?"

They moved out onto the terrace for coffee and afterwards Eve insisted on helping him clear the table. He was enormously efficient, she noted, very methodical, a perfectionist in everything he did.

"Come and listen to some music," he said, folding his arms around her, his breath fragrant with coffee.

"That's what you always say." She leaned back into his embrace.

"I don't want to appear too obsessed with getting you into bed."

"But you are."

"Would you like me to sweep you up right now?" he challenged her.

"You're a man to die for, Drew," she sighed, instantly intensely aroused.

"So how come you can resist me?" His voice was a little rough, a faint tremor in his strong arms.

"I've got a lot of trauma in my head," she told him with a catch.

"Such is the irony. I could have picked a dozen beautiful women."

"You must have stopped counting." She reached back, touched his cheek.

"So why do I lust after you?" he asked in a low, vibrant voice. She gave a little shudder at his words and he bent and kissed the side of her silky ear. "Only joking. You've lifted the curtain of love for me, Eve. I'm not just talking about sexual feelings. Come and join me on the sofa. I have something for you."

She looked up at him with widened eyes. "What could it possibly be?"

"Hang on. I'll get it." He walked off towards the

master bedroom, turning on the CD player in the state-of-the-art entertainment unit as he went.

Anne-Sophie Mutter on violin playing with the Berlin Philharmonic, the "Romance" CD Eve loved. She slipped off her low-heeled suede shoes, pushed up the long sleeves of her thin V-neck burgundy sweater she wore with matching slacks, and sat down on a sofa, resting her head on the wonderfully plush arm.

When Drew returned he had removed his jacket and tie and was carrying a small luxuriously wrapped gift parcel in his hand.

Eve sat up quickly, tossing back her long hair. "Have all my birthdays come at once?"

"You're just an out-and-out adorable girl," he mocked, instead of handing her the parcel, putting it down just out of reach on the coffee table and pulling her into his arms.

"I have a powerful urge to protect you, Evie," he said.

"You don't think I can look after myself?"

"You can. Extremely well. By the same token it's taken its toll. I think you deserve to be pampered for a while."

"Lovely!" She stretched out her arms, the movement pulling the fine wool taut across her breasts.

It was like a switch had been thrown in his head. With a deep primitive sound even resembling a growl, he lowered his head, his eyes extravagantly dark with desire.

He kissed her deeply, so deeply Eve thought he might steal her soul. She would never get over the shock of his wanting her, the never to be borne excitement of having his hands rove her. Her legs and the toes of her feet stretched in a kind of agony. She was softly moaning as if she were on a rack, but a rack so exquisite it stretched her to incredible yearning.

"Drew." She only just managed to free the mouth that was pressed to his. "I'll *die* if you don't stop."

"But I haven't touched you yet." He eased a voluptuous hand down over her clothed body, his handsome face taut with his own passion. "I don't believe I made love to a woman before you," he said in wonderment. "You're the woman I knew existed but couldn't find. Are you scared?" He stared down into her liquid green eyes.

"Yes." When her arms were knotted around his neck.

"This might panic you even more." He reached for the packet, placing it on her lap. "Open it, Eve. I want to see your face."

While the beautiful music filled the room, Eve pulled the ribbons off the package and opened up the silver, green-medallion-embossed paper, careful not to tear it. An exquisite porcelain box was inside, executed in golds and enamels with stones that surely couldn't be emeralds, surrounding a watercolour of a lovely young woman with swirling blond hair on the lid.

"Oh, Drew, this is too extravagant for me," she protested as soon as her eyes fell on it, but her face reflected her delight. "They're surely not emeralds?" She traced the small glittering stones with a delicate finger.

"Colombian. What's more, it dates from the turn of the century. I couldn't resist it. The girl could be you. It's actually a music box. If you turn the little key on the back it plays an old French song. 'Plaisir d'Amour.'" He began to hum a snatch of it, stopping when Eve got the music box working.

"I love it. I absolutely love it," she said. "You want to be careful. I'll cry. You're so kind."

"It's not *kindness* that inspired me, my love," he said in a dark, wry voice. "Open it up."

"Don't tell me there's more?"

With a tremendous shock that elicited a sharply indrawn breath, Eve saw slotted into the midnight-blue velvet the most beautiful diamond and platinum engagement ring she had ever seen in her life and she had seen a good many from her time working in the jewellery shop. The central stone was of superb colour and clarity, easily two carats, flanked by smaller diamonds of the same rose cut. Eve stared at it spellbound. She even tried to speak without success. The golden glow from a table lamp fell directly on the stones so they flashed out mesmerising beams of light. Her heart was thudding so painfully she thought she was about to faint.

"I knew you'd be surprised," Drew said to her in a voice that came close to self-mockery.

"Drew, is this for me?" From the expression on her face she might have been Cinderella.

"Was I wrong to think you clever?" he teased.

"An engagement ring?" She felt thrilled, excited, but committed to an answer. Wasn't that the purpose of an engagement ring?

"It is and it's particularly beautiful, don't you think?"

"The most beautiful I've ever seen." It dazzled and blazed. "It must have cost an awful lot of money."

"It doesn't matter," he said with a faint smile. "I want you to have the best. Here, let me take it out before you shut it away again. You're not just mine, Evie, to love and touch. I want us to get married. I want us to be together for the rest of our lives. I know you're haunted by the past, your mother's broken heart, but this is *us*. Our life. Your engagement ring is my vow of commitment. I swear I'll never break it."

The whole thing had the quality of some beautiful dream.

"I don't know if I could stand it if you did."

"Have faith, my love. We'll conquer your fears together."

Drew slipped the glorious ring down over Evie's finger. "You're mine now, Evie, to love and to honour."

She stared back into his handsome dark face.

"You truly believe this is destined?"

"Don't you?"

"I so want to," she whispered. "It's wonderful when we're together. But marriage is such a perilous journey."

"My darling, you relish a challenge." He put his arms around her, feeling her heart beat through her breast. She clung to him as he kissed her hair, her temple, her cheek. "What's it to be, Evie?"

"No one in the world would expect you to marry me," she sighed deeply.

"I don't know if I can follow that."

"Well, your background." She rested against him. "I've never been part of your world."

"I notice you haven't had the least trouble moving in it," he said soothingly. "Nothing you can say will put me off, Evie. Only the words, *I don't love you.* Can you honestly say them?"

She felt she was a sobbing little girl again, pounding at her father. "I would never be in your bed if I didn't care about you deeply, Drew. You know that."

"But love is the forbidden word?"

"I recognise that myself." Her face was hidden by a veil of gold.

"But you'll agree to marry me? It might sound like undue persuasion, but there are many ways I can help

Ben.'' His voice had a faint bite of satire. ''You're not the sort of woman to be a sex object, Evie. We should get married, the way we feel.''

Didn't she know it in her heart? ''It's worse for a woman, Drew,'' she said, too long a witness to her mother's grief.

''I don't believe that's true.'' Drew tightened his hold on her. ''I've known men devastated by marriage break-downs. Indeed suicidal, especially when there are children involved. The courts inevitably grant custody to the mother. I know your mind is always drawn irresistibly to your parents, but you're not looking at the full picture. You have to get rid of your doubts now. If you don't, they'll destroy you. Let me love you, Evie. I'll atone for it all.''

The flow of words ceased as he bent over her, gathered her up into his arms and held her tight against his heart.

That night their lovemaking went beyond the bounds of sensory rapture entering the realm of the sublime as though each knew only in the other would they become whole. Nothing was held back. Where Drew led, Eve followed, rising to his immense desire, matching him, until the flame burned so bright it devoured them in its radiant heat. This was one dream that had come true.

Afterwards as they lay limbs entwined, spent with joy, the phone on the bedside table rang. ''Don't answer it,'' Eve whispered, then her mind inevitably jumped to Ben in hospital. ''Better, I suppose.''

His answer was swift and warm. ''Relax, Ben's okay.''

He was a mind reader.

''Forsythe,'' Drew answered. There was a silence. Eventually he said. ''Tomorrow is out I'm afraid, Susan.

It's a full day but what about Wednesday? Say 1:00 p.m. at Carrington's?''

Eve who had been lying languidly on her side, one arm flung across his chest, spontaneously pulled away.

*Don't do this,* she thought, trying to get a rein on her dismay. Don't spoil this precious time.

"Evie, what is it?'' Drew asked after he replaced the receiver. Though he wrapped one arm around her silken body, she sat up on the side of the bed.

"Why would she be ringing you this time of night?'' Eve was demanding. She was completely naked, her beautiful skin suffused with the honey glow from the lamp. His mind leapt to some love verses from Solomon and his satiated body stirred in renewed desire. "It has to be getting on for eleven o'clock.''

"She did apologise,'' Drew answered mildly. "She's just come in from a friend's. Eve, I don't want you to leave me tonight.''

"I think I'd better.'' Though she was doing her level best to fight it off, Eve felt emotionally chilled.

"Eve.'' Drew's warm, seductive voice turned hard. "Don't do this.''

"All right, let's talk about *Susan.*'' She turned on him, her expression quite passionate.

Drew looked at her searchingly. She was outraged. "I'd be pleased to, if only you'll come back here beside me.'' He didn't wait for her answer, but drew her without warning back into his bed. "Angel,'' was what he murmured. "Don't let Susan disrupt the wonderful memory of tonight.''

It was exactly her own thoughts. But she had to *know.* "What does she want with you, Drew?'' she asked huskily, lying over on her back and staring up into his face.

"She's going through a bad time, Evie." He took her hand and kissed the tips of her fingers gently.

"I know that, but I need to understand *exactly* why. She's mourning your father, but I feel I have to tell you she's more taken up with you than you realise."

"Oh, God. I guess so. Increased dependency, I suppose. She needs a shoulder to cry on."

Eve came to life with sudden passion. "Not yours," she cried, suddenly pummelling him. "You've just taken on a fiancée."

"So I have!" He gave an aroused laugh, grasping her by the shoulders and landed an almost savage kiss on her mouth. It stopped Eve's struggling and kept her silent for quite a few moments after. "Susan is my father's widow," Drew finally explained, putting an arm beneath her head. "She needs me at the moment. I can't just bundle her out of my life."

"I understand that, but you can't realise how obsessed she is with you," Eve said anxiously.

"Evie, please give me a chance," Drew begged. "My father was a businessman before he was anything else. He had a prenuptial agreement drawn up prior to the marriage. Susan signed it."

"I don't believe it."

Eve sounded so shocked, Drew's mouth quirked. "It's true."

"That wasn't terribly kind, let alone romantic. You must let me know if I'm supposed to sign one."

Drew laughed. "Dad wasn't a great romantic, Evie. He was a hard-headed realist. Susan has been very well provided for. But I'm my father's heir. Family assets remain within the family. That was Dad's credo."

"So Susan wasn't *family?*" Eve's voice was ironical.

"I agree it's hard—" Drew stroked her shoulder

"—but Dad and Susan made their own arrangement. Each had something the other wanted. The thing that upset me is, something happened before Dad's death. Something that created a great deal of tension. Susan blames herself."

"Perhaps she has reason to." Eve's attitude was quieter now. She still retained the memory of Susan's face when she had surprised them in the library the night of the Capricornia party. Brilliant as he was, it was perfectly possible Drew had unconsciously turned a *blind* eye to Susan's deepening feelings. It was his way of respecting his father's marriage.

"The house is mine," he told Eve now.

"You mean, Susan has to go?" Eve tipped back her head to stare into his eyes.

"That's what makes it sad. I feel sorry for her. Dad might have left it to her in her lifetime but he regarded it as the *family* home."

"And Susan wasn't family, of course." Eve echoed her earlier comment wryly.

Drew shook his head. "It's a fact of life marriages break down. Maybe Dad was haunted by the fact Susan was half his age."

Eve settled her head deeper into his shoulder, letting a moment pass. "She did try to have a baby."

"I wish she had succeeded," Drew said. "It would have given her something to live for. All I've ever offered Susan is comfort, Evie. You are going to have to accept that once and for all."

Eve reached up to press a kiss on his chin. "Forgive me, I'm just the poor old victim of a damaged childhood. I hate all my own doubts, Drew. I hate the things I say to you. But you can't afford to be too off guard around Susan. She's pushing for a relationship."

"No!" Drew's denial was taut. "For God's sake, Evie. That's truly impossible. Even if *you* were Susan, I couldn't marry my father's widow." He broke off, his expression stark. "Hell, I wouldn't like to be faced with that one. Susan is beautiful, intelligent, refined. I've always found her sweet and gentle. She'll remarry. I don't think there's any doubt about that. Dad left her a rich woman."

"And you're having lunch Wednesday?" She was hideously aware her tone was dry.

"She doesn't want to stay in the house though I offered it to her for as long as she liked," Drew explained. "She wants to move out."

"I'm sympathetic to that. Where to?"

"Now here's the dilemma." Drew's tone combined genuine unease with involuntary black humour.

"I just knew there'd be one. They don't seem to go away." Eve manoeuvred herself out of the bed, reached for Drew's dark ruby robe and put it on.

"You look wonderful in that." Drew let his eyes run up and down her body, wondering why he had never seen her in that deep rich colour. She was all ruby, alabaster and gold, her eyes as jewel-like as the emeralds on the porcelain box.

"Don't change the subject, Drew," she warned him.

There was a slight look of strain in Drew's eyes. "I don't *want* to. I don't need Susan on my doorstep, but she's shown a lot of interest in the penthouse unit beside this, as have a lot of people, I should add. If she's serious, I can't stop her buying. It's well known Ian Fraser is about to put it on the market."

"And Ian Fraser is a good friend of yours, isn't he? You could stitch up a deal over drinks."

"Possibly." Drew sensed he was losing ground. "But

even if Susan did buy, I wouldn't be remaining here long. As soon as Susan vacates the house I'll move in. I'd like to live there, unless you have something else in mind.''

"Nope," Eve said sharply. "Meanwhile you can buddy up with Susan?''

"You're jealous. I love it!'' Drew raised mocking brows.

"No, no, jealousy has nothing to do with it. It's simply not an arrangement that suits me.'' Susan at the door, run out of sugar. A few friends are coming for dinner, you must join us. Stay on for a nightcap. It was exactly what Drew needed to avoid.

"There should be a whole lot more fiancées just like you,'' he laughed. "Seems like you're trying to protect your man.''

"I sure am.'' An answering flash of humour crossed Eve's face. "I'm having enough problems letting our engagement sink in. I never set out to marry the boss. I was totally in awe of you at the beginning.''

"Easy, Eve. Don't lie. You let me know I was far from perfect the very first day.''

The very first day he made her knees weak. "When do you want to get married?'' she asked, giving him the sweetest of smiles.

"That's better,'' he murmured. "Much better. As soon as possible. I want us to be together morning, noon and night. Live in a haven of love. The full mourning period for Dad isn't quite up. How does late September sound to you? A spring bride.''

A spring bride! The very thought filled her with elation, excitement and at another level, extreme agitation, and it couldn't be denied. She was, or she had been, an organised working girl. A career woman performing very well at a high executive level. How would she go as a wife? She had quite a few hang-ups to handle. Everyone had such wonderful dreams to start with. Her own mother had had such hopes, but there were dangers pressing in from all sides. Why, when she was so confident in her work, did she have such a terror of failure?

"I figure out I could do with an answer." Drew smiled.

"Don't you think we need more time?"

"Just look at me," Drew said, lounging so gracefully, so arousingly, in the bed. The white sheet was pulled taut across his lean hips, the light gilding his bronzed shoulders and chest. "Does it make any sense our being apart?"

Eve stabbed a hand through her long hair. "Couples live together. That kind of thing."

"Sorry, Evie." He slanted her a short burning look. "It's not on. I want you for my *wife*. After we're married we can live together."

She stared back at him, saw the devilment that was always in his dark eyes.

"I didn't say you have to give up your career, though I'd hope you'd want children, as well."

"Of course." Eve whirled to face him directly. "I'll adore any children we have." She walked back to the bed and sat down on the side of it. "Being realistic, I couldn't walk off and leave a small child. That would make us all unhappy. But at some stage I think I could manage both a family and a career. I'm supposed to be an achiever, after all."

"Evie, darling, you are." Drew touched her shoulders tenderly, then drew his robe slowly down her slender arms. "I don't doubt between the two of us we'll manage."

"Oh, God, Drew," she said as he began to caress her. Her body was like hot wax under his hands. She could feel herself melting.

"I told you I'm not letting you go home."

"You'd rather we walk out together in broad daylight."

"Have you forgotten? You're my fiancée."

Any other protest was drowned by the sheer power of desire.

# CHAPTER NINE

DREW'S and Eve's engagement was not received with universal delight. Susan and Carol were shocked. And they weren't alone. Any number of women had their noses out of joint. Who was Eve Copeland, anyway? An employee? Someone who worked on financial strategies? There were plenty of well-bred, eligible young women who had known Drew from childhood. Any one of them could have made Drew Forsythe a suitable wife. Drew was enormously rich. Enormously handsome. Enormously popular. It was unbelievable he would consider marrying a young woman of no established background. No name. No position in society. A young woman, moreover, he had known for less than a year.

It was Carol once again who tried to make the most trouble, getting the gossip going, peppering it with half truths, half lies. In her unprecedented jealousy she even moved closer to Susan, who herself was filled with a terrible black dismay, but blessed with the sense to hide it.

Sitting over lunch close after the formal announcement had been made, Carol tried to prod Susan into some satisfactory reaction. It wasn't enough to see her hands shaking badly.

"Of course she was after him from day one." Carol's voice was cold. "That's why these girls get their fancy business degrees, so they can go after their bosses."

"I'm sure it wasn't like that, Carol," Susan said. "I

understand Eve had an excellent job with Pearce Musgrave.''

"And who, pray, is Pierce Musgrave?" Carol asked haughtily, then pushed the salt away. "Oh, Pearce Musgrave the merchant bank! I'm not sure I see that as a wonderful recommendation. She has no parents. Did you know that?''

Susan shook her dark head, wondering why she had come. "She has a father, but apparently she doesn't see him. Her parents divorced when Eve and her brother were quite young. Her mother unfortunately was killed in a road accident.''

"So it's just like I said. She has *nobody*.''

"She has Drew," Susan cut in very brusquely, then made quite an effort to modify her tone. "Hasn't she?''

"Sure." Carol sighed in exasperation. "You can't fool me, Susan. You're as upset as I am.''

"I can't think the marriage will happen, that's why.''

"A million bucks it does," Carol said emphatically. "Unless we do something about it.''


Ben, too, though prepared, was nevertheless stunned at the speed of events. Since childhood he and Evie had been so very close, now another man had entered Evie's life. Much as he liked and admired Drew, Drew was such a dynamic character, Ben thought, he could put a gap between himself and his sister. Much as he tried to hide it, Ben felt sad. Emotional attachments are the very devil, he thought. In many ways Eve had been more of a mother to him than the woman who had borne them both.

"We want you to come and live with us while you're doing all your studying," Eve told him one night as they were watching TV.

"Wh-a-a-t!" Ben who was comfortably lounging, sat up straight. "Hell, Evie, that's an awful idea."

"Awful?" Eve looked back at her brother in amazement. "I think it's great. Drew wants to talk to you about it."

Ben found the remote control and turned off the television. "Your husband-to-be, who incidentally is mad about you, has no objections to taking in your brother?" He gave a short laugh. "You're kidding."

"Heck, Ben, this is a surprise. I thought you'd be pleased."

"I can fend for myself, Evie." Unfortunately it wasn't strictly true. Drew had already helped. In lots of ways.

"Two's company, three's a crowd. Especially with newly married couples."

Eve showed him a deeply disappointed face. "Gosh, Ben, we won't be in one another's pockets. You'll see the house on Saturday night. It's *huge*. My first tiff with Drew and I wouldn't have to lay eyes on him for a week. Anyway, we thought you would want your own privacy. There's a self-contained flat that was often used by guests. It has its own entry. It even has its own garage. I've seen over it. I'm sure you'd love it. You'd be very comfortable and private when you wanted to be. You can invite your own friends."

Ben held his head briefly. "You're telling me Drew genuinely wants this?"

"Ben, dear," Eve said gently, "I can swear to it. Whether you like it or not, you've got a big brother."

"And you didn't try to fix it?" Ben looked at her with searching hazel eyes.

"Lord, no." Eve held his gaze. "Naturally I want you close to me and I want you to be happy. You'll be moving off soon enough, Benjamin Copeland, M.D."

"I'm not sure, Evie." Ben turned the television back on, all of a sudden looking a lot brighter. "Let me think it over."

"It will be hard to disappoint Drew," was all Eve said.

The following Saturday night was the engagement party or the "shindig" as Ben kept referring to it. It was to be held at the Forsythe family home, with Drew already in residence. One hundred guests had been invited. Eve's own list had amounted to no more than fifteen. Mostly friends and partners from her university days. Lisa, of course. And Ben. All the rest were Drew's extended family and friends.

Eve spent two hours getting ready, her excitement a little clouded by nerves. So many people would be looking at her, assessing her, making their judgments. They'd never heard of her, of course. Could this marriage work? Susan would be there. They could hardly have left out Sir David's widow. Susan, who had left rather a large hole in her bank account buying the penthouse apartment to capture a highly elusive prey.

Now Drew was in residence in his old family home and he and Eve were engaged. Though some people didn't look on marriage as binding, let alone an engagement, Eve thought wryly. Drew was a man for whom any woman would risk getting burned. At last she was dressed, staring at herself very critically in the mirrored doors of her wardrobe. She had made up her face a little more than usual. Eyes, mouth, the extra shimmer of special foundation. Her blond hair had been dressed high and away from her face by Raymond, a long gleaming bell that fell smoothly over her shoulders. If all eyes were going to be fixed on her, they wouldn't be able to fault her appearance. Her dress was lovely, shimmering, strapless, bead-encrusted pale green chiffon.

"Yes, yes, yes, a Grace Kelly kind of dress!" Lisa had exclaimed as soon as the boutique owner returned with it over her arm. They had almost settled on a beautiful spring floral but when Eve tried the gown on there was no question about which one to buy.

When she went into the living room, Ben, wonderfully attractive in the first formal clothes of his life, a beautifully cut dinner suit and black tie, gave a long almost soundless whistle.

"Evie, you look gorgeous! Where did you find that dress? It's terrific." His eyes moved over her with brotherly pride. "There won't be a woman in the place to touch you."

"I don't know about that. Lisa will come close. And you haven't met Lady Forsythe yet." Her faint smile was unbearably touched with an element of worry.

"Aphrodite could turn up and Drew wouldn't see her. He only has eyes for you, Evie. I know what you're going through," he said in a low warm voice. "What happened to Mum invaded every aspect of our lives. But you're so much *more* than our poor little mother, Evie. We loved her a lot, but both of us knew she wasn't a survivor. She didn't have solutions. She never tried to work any out. *You* were the one who was always pushing on with what had to be done. You were the one who had to handle me. I was in a pretty bad way, too, after Dad left. You're a strong individual, Evie. And you're clever. You can hold on to any man."

"Even Drew?"

"Sure. So don't go worrying yourself about *permanence* when you've only just got engaged. Marry him. Make it work."

"Or call the whole thing off." Eve suddenly laughed, reached up and patted her brother's cheek. "Thanks, Ben. I'm glad you're going to be there tonight."

It had been arranged they would arrive early, before the guests, and while Ben explored the house, professing from the outset he had fallen in love with it, Drew drew Eve into the library, so delighted with her appearance his dark eyes burned with sexual intensity. "I haven't given you my engagement present yet."

"You have, *too!*" Bubbling with excitement Evie held up her glittering left hand, smiling at him with such sweetness it was all he could do not to sweep her up and carry her away.

"I want to give you *more,*" he said.

"But, Drew, I have nothing." She had given him several small presents from time to time, wondering all the while what you gave a man who had everything.

"You're all I'll ever need and want," Drew pointed out gently. "My mother left a good deal of jewellery. All of it is yours. But I want you to wear my gift tonight. It will go perfectly with that dress."

"Drew, you're spoiling me. Truly." Eve's voice sounded a little odd.

"Don't cry, darling," Drew warned her. "Don't ruin your makeup." His hand brushed her shoulders. He wanted desperately to kiss her but held back.

"That's as good a warning as any."

Eve held her breath as Drew produced a long dark green velvet box. "Turn round," he ordered.

Eve did, feeling swept away.

"Maybe you'd better hold your hair away for a moment."

"Very well." She put up her hands and lifted her hair from her fine, smooth neck.

A moment more and Drew placed a string of pearls around it, a heart-shaped, diamond-encrusted pendant sitting perfectly against her skin.

"Could I look?" Eve fingered the diamond pendant, suddenly terribly aware of the role she was being cast in. From rags to riches, she thought incredulously. No, not rags, never rags, but there had never been much money to spare. Now this. In marrying Drew, overnight she would become a very rich woman. She wouldn't be an ordinary person at all. Doing ordinary things. She wasn't so sure of herself that she didn't think it was scary.

Drew led her by the hand to a gilded Regency mirror on top of a carved console.

"Like it?" He bent to her reflection.

"*Love* it." Eve had to distract herself so as not to cry. The pearls were lustrous orbs, the diamond heart below them glittered like a starburst. It wasn't easy, she discovered, being showered with gifts.

"You'll have to take off your earrings," he said softly. "Not that they don't look lovely, but these match the necklace." He held up a pair of earrings and lights flashed.

"I don't deserve you," Evie said, certain it was true. "I don't deserve all this kindness."

He made a little scoffing sound. "I told you before, Evie, kindness has nothing to do with it. These come with all my love."

Strong emotion kicked up inside her.

"You're not going to cry, are you?"

"No, I'm not. Don't worry about me. I'm fine." She

was absurdly happy, her heart racing a thousand beats to the minute.

The earrings were exquisite. Small diamond hearts hung from single large perfect pearls.

After she had fixed them, Drew put his hands over her delicate shoulders, his fingers moving caressingly along her collarbone. "Want to show Ben? I want to kiss you so badly, if we don't move I just might lose the struggle." Yet he looked arresting, a man of extraordinary male beauty, perfectly in control of himself except for the faint tremor in his strong hands.

"You look marvellous," Eve said, mesmerised by their reflections, Drew with his dark colouring, the raven hair, the eyes, and bronzed skin, she looking more like a figurine in cream and gold.

"This is our night, Evie," he said, and gripped her hand.

Thus armed, Eve went out to greet the first of their guests already at the front door. If Drew thought she was very special. She was.

The party developed beautifully. Although there were many older guests, most were Drew's friends, all around his age. Quite a few had returned home from overseas postings, Eve found. She, who had decided she was going to take it easy and enjoy herself, was delighted to meet so many friendly, lively and stimulating people who seemed just as delighted to meet her and make her one of them.

"You two are going to be perfect, I just know," Luke Farrell, one of Drew's closest friends, told her.

That seemed to be the consensus of opinion.

Ben, too, was having the time of his life, looking older than his twenty years and very handsome in his dinner clothes. More than one young woman had rushed up to him, seduced by his golden good looks and not taking terribly much notice of the pert brunette called Lisa who kept jumping in the way.

Susan was there, gowned and coiffured to perfection, her tall willowy figure shown off to its best advantage in a long sapphire blue gown only a favoured few could possibly wear. Charity work dominated her time. A constant round of functions. She wanted to devote time to the less fortunate, she told everyone in her soft charming tones.

"Face it, isn't that most of us?" Lisa quipped irreverently.

All through the evening Drew was never more than a few feet from Eve's side. Even then he kept moving back to her, profoundly pleased with her impact on his friends. Happiness made her blond beauty incandescent but her bright conversation kept their guests clustered around her.

"Ah, now I understand how she landed him," an older male relative of Drew's whispered in Susan's ear, never dreaming she was seething with upset. "She's really quite delightful and the IQ shows. Apart from her looks, I always found Carol deadly dull."

Isn't anyone aware how I feel? Susan thought. This used to be *my* home. I was a brilliant hostess. I was married to the richest man in this state. Now I'm a widow, a woman on my own, forced to take a back seat. Why? She had a cool and ruthless head. She knew how to seduce a man.

Susan was ashamed of the terrible thoughts that invaded her mind. Was she sick to even think of them? Yet every day her feelings for Drew were becoming more obsessive. She realised that just as she realised she had lost the power to control the situation.

Revelation came to her in a blinding flash. It rocked her to her core.

*She had never told Drew how she felt.* He didn't even *know* she loved him. She had hidden it from him.

Fool! She would do anything now to have him for herself.

Drew. The incomparable Drew.

Shed this madness, the sane voice inside her warned. But the force of obsession drove her on.

Eve was never sure how it happened, but as the weeks flew by and the work on the Capricornia project was stepped up, Susan somehow managed to ingratiate herself as Eve's would-be mentor. Eve had been prepared for some sort of interference but Susan was so persuasive and pleasant they had somehow come to having weekly lunch together.

"Of course, the big day is going to be a marvellous occasion—" Susan smiled "—but there are a great many anxieties and pressures along the way. Let me ease your path, Eve, and help you keep calm. After all, you're working so hard, it must be hard to focus on two things at once."

"There's a *lot* happening, Susan." Eve was beginning to feel quite uncomfortable. "Capricornia has to come in on time and we're working against the wet season. There are very many projects out there. The partners are getting together for Mount Maratta. Drew is working especially hard."

Susan reached across the small window table and patted Eve's hand. "My dear, Drew can cope. He was bred to it. But this is a very big challenge for such a young woman. I've been there. I know how it's all done. *Trust me.*"

It was hard to deal with such a sticky situation especially when Susan kept talking endlessly.

"—You have to have *someone* to help you. After all, I am 'family.' I'd love it if you got into the habit of discussing things with me. Don't think you have to bottle up your problems."

"There is Drew," Eve pointed out deftly. "A big wedding is a challenge, I admit, but I'm a good organiser."

"I'm sure you are." Susan worked hard to smile. "The thing is, Eve, you'll be helping *me*. I've been so unhappy since I lost David. You'll take my mind off my grief."

"Susan wants to help me find my wedding dress," Eve confided to Lisa over the phone.

"You're not going to let her?" Lisa all but shrieked.

"Of course I'm not." Eve clicked her tongue. "I don't want to create any upsets, either. Drew's not good at being unkind to women. He gets fed up from time to time, but basically he's sympathetic towards Susan's position. God knows why, but I think he feels he owes her."

"Well, its common knowledge Drew got the lion's share of everything," Lisa pointed out. "And she's particularly sweet around him, men love women who need caring for. Actually, I didn't take to her at all," Lisa confessed. "It's amazing but I thought she's got more than a touch of the Wicked Queen. You know, 'Mirror, mirror on the wall' and so forth. In fact I'm not absolutely certain she doesn't want Drew for herself. Perhaps a touch incestuous."

"And painful," Eve said. "It might be easier to elope."

"No way!" Lisa, the chief bridesmaid, swiftly vetoed that. "Tell Susan, the hoity-toity Lady Forsythe, you'll do very nicely without her."

Despite her best efforts, and Eve had learned to take quite a lot on board, it was becoming increasingly difficult to plan the perfect wedding to the extent she was starting to feel pressured. She didn't have a fiancé who could take time off to sit down with her and plan exactly what they wanted. Drew, above all, was TCR's chief executive officer with all that implied.

"You could take time off," Drew suggested when she brought up the subject, "only you're too close to the action. Frankly I can't do without you until we get a few things like Maratta and the Austral venture out of the way. You're very patient and cool when it comes to closing finances. What we really need is a support system," he joked.

"We do." Eve took it seriously. "I have no family."

"What about Susan?" Drew nodded towards his secretary, who was wanting him to sign papers. "She might enjoy the job. She's been very unhappy of late."

"I'm sure I told you she has offered to help," Eve murmured dryly, all of which appeared to go over Drew's sleek dark head.

"Then why not let her check out a few things?" He finished what he was doing, smiled at Sara.

"Like book the honeymoon?" Despite herself Eve's words came out almost combative.

Drew paused, looked up at her, dark eyes suddenly gleaming. "Oh, I think we can organise that ourselves. You, me, on a magical desert island. No phones. No TV.

No one to reach us. We can wave at the ships going by. And frankly, my love, I can't wait. Why don't you draw up a checklist of things Susan might be able to do? The time-consuming things you can't get round to. We have the final say. Susan was good at organising parties and functions for Dad. She could help enormously if you let her. It might be a kindness.''

Kindness or not, Eve didn't want Susan taking a hand in anything. Eve felt under the soft, cultivated facade there was envy as dark as night. As the bride-to-be, Eve soon found it was easy to plunge from the dizzy heights of rapture to the depths of distress. Even Ben was asking her if she could cope.

Seeing this, Susan decided it was time for the next move. ''You're looking a little pressured, Eve,'' she said sympathetically the next time they had lunch. In fact, being in love had given an extra dimension to the girl's fine-featured beauty. She was wearing a very elegant black suit and it added drama to her cream and gold colouring.

''There are always problems, Susan,'' Eve said, making up her mind she would have something else to do at lunchtimes in future.

''I know just how you feel.'' Susan picked up her menu and scanned it sightlessly before putting it down. ''Before I was married, I continually worried if I could measure up as David's wife. You must feel exactly the same with Drew?''

Eve didn't hesitate. ''To be perfectly honest, I don't think I'll have any trouble at all. Drew is enormously supportive.''

''Ah, how well I know that!'' Susan sighed. ''He's been kindness itself to me.''

"Well, of course." Eve had to acknowledge it. "He lost a father. You lost a husband. It's very sad."

"Oh, it began long before then." Susan looked away, her eyes clouding in remembrance. "Drew was an ally right from the beginning."

"It's no secret he really does try to help people," Eve said, keeping her voice even.

"Of course he was trying to get over the effects of Carol then. That marriage should have never happened. I just knew it wouldn't work."

"Why is that?" Eve was determined to get it out of her.

"Well, for one thing, the more time he spent with her Drew realised she just couldn't measure up. She—"

"I'm not sure what you mean?" Eve interrupted her.

"Well, there's no denying Carol is very glamorous and sexy but to put it bluntly she wasn't the right woman for Drew to have at his side." Susan spoke out of a deeply felt jealousy.

"And you were?"

Before she even knew what she was doing, Susan nodded then flushed violently in reaction.

"You're in love with him, aren't you?" Eve asked, showing more pity than anything else.

Susan's large blue eyes seemed to focus on her with difficulty. "I probably shouldn't say it but there was a time…" She broke off, tears filling her eyes.

"Don't stop."

"I think we should leave it."

"No, lets deal with it right now. There was a time…"

"Didn't you recognise it yourself?" Susan issued the soft challenge.

"I've been expecting this." Sadly, Eve shook her head.

"We women can't fool one another," Susan said rue-
fully. "I don't threaten you, Eve. I fully sympathise with
your position. You sensed very early Drew and I are
very close. I married his father, true. We tried to make
a life together. A life that was over almost as soon as it
began. David, too, sensed the strong bond between myself and Drew. We argued that last night. I never saw
David alive again."

"Are you going to tell me about the argument, too?"
Eve heard the irony in her own voice.

"Much better I don't." Susan looked away. A woman
with secrets.

"What an extraordinary woman you are, Susan."

"I've always seen myself as that."

"And it's your intention to try and drive a wedge
between Drew and me?"

"I'm trying to tell you about something that's hidden.
You may marry Drew, Eve, but I think you realise I'll
always be there in the background."

"As what?" Eve asked almost encouragingly.

"As something we can never show to the world.
Much as he cares about me, Drew knows society would
never accept me as his wife. In becoming Lady Forsythe
I forfeited my chances." Susan's voice faded with the
realisation the price had been too much.

"It's a delusion, of course," Eve said simply. "The
impossible dream. You have to wave goodbye to it,
Susan. Go for a long trip overseas. Save your sanity.
Think of any story you like. Take yourself off. I don't
want you around to spoil our big day."

When Eve returned to the office, many emotions flowing
through her, it was to find Drew making preparations to
go to the $406-million Sunderland copper-gold mine

where trouble was brewing. The local aboriginal people had sought an injunction to halt operations, arguing they had been denied their rights under native title. The government and TCR, who held the lease, were arguing no native title existed, but it was clear it was in the interests of all parties that a resolution be reached. Emotions were running high. Mine management stated the native title claims were simply vexatious, which the other side rejected. Drew intended to leave the following morning and take Rhys Thomas, QC, the company counsel, along. The case had already been put to the federal court with the judge reserving his decision. As a consequence, operations were continuing, but in a state of flux. It wasn't time to talk about Susan.

Eve returned to the house with Drew that evening. She had been getting to know this large mansion, walking around it at her leisure, gradually deciding if there was anything she wanted to change. As far as Drew was concerned this would be her home and she had carte blanche to redecorate if she so wished. Certain aspects of the house were Susan, and Eve thought she might change some, though very gradually. There would be plenty of time to settle into this most beautiful of homes.

While Drew finished off some work in his study, Eve walked into the kitchen, made coffee and took it into him. They had eaten earlier at a small restaurant, now Drew wanted a few hours alone with her to relax.

"There are no risks involved, I hope?" Eve asked with a pang of anxiety. She was seated on the green leather sofa, looking towards Drew at his desk.

"Tempers are flaring, that's all." Drew shook his dark head. "It will be an intolerable situation if operations are brought to a halt. The answer, quite obviously, is face-to-face mediation. We're not about riding roughshod over legitimate claims. Our intention is to be strictly fair in our dealings. We've honoured land rights in the past. I'm sure with goodwill on both sides we'll work it out. Anyway, enough of that, I just want to be with you. That's what matters the most. Our being together.''

Drew stood up, walked over to the chesterfield and scooped her up. He bent his head and brushed his mouth lightly, shiveringly, back and forth over hers. "How long do we have to wait?"

"Not quite six weeks," she sighed. "The invitations have gone. I don't think we'll get any refusals. Maybe Susan." Her mouth turned down wryly.

"Susan? Why, what's the matter?" Still holding her, Drew sank back in an armchair.

"I think she has some idea of going overseas." Eve decided to gloss over Susan quickly.

"This is the first I've heard about it. I thought she was being a lot of help to you."

"Actually no!" Eve tipped back her head, her emotions more tangled than she thought.

"Is there something going on I don't know about?"

"Oh, please, don't let's talk about Susan," Eve moaned. "I wish I'd never laid eyes on the woman."

"But obviously we must." Drew managed a twisted smile. "Has she upset you in some way?"

"You're dead right," she said quietly when she wanted to shout.

"So, I'm asking, what did she say?" Drew closed a hand around her nape.

"Give me a break!" Suddenly, Eve was at flashpoint. Her heart beat like thunder. She jerked away, curling into a tight defensive position on another armchair. "You've heard every word of it before."

"Evie!" Looking completely baffled, Drew threw up his hands. "It's been a long day. What the hell's wrong?"

"Oh, God, I don't know." She couldn't diagnose her own mood. "I'm more difficult than most, I suppose."

"Your surely not suggesting you're having second thoughts?"

What an absurd idea! Still she lost her head, in fact, said something hurtful and stupid. "You haven't given me much time."

"No." Danger and turbulence prowled in his dark eyes. "But you *agreed* to marry me. You made a commitment. A *commitment,* Evie. Isn't that something you're big on?" he asked harshly even as he thought, What am I doing? This woman he loved had such a tragic history.

"I didn't mean—" Eve started, then closed her eyes.

"Tell me, then. What *do* you mean?" Drew begged.

Her beautiful eyes flew open, burning green. "Did you ever give Susan the *slightest* encouragement?"

Drew groaned aloud. Finally, he thought he'd lost it. "Do you enjoy doing this?" he demanded. "I've given you all the comfort and reassurance I know how. I took your hand. Put my ring on it. What can I possibly do more?"

Eve could feel herself trembling. "You can answer my question."

The bright light shone on Drew's taut, striking face. "There's no need," he rasped.

"Then how am I supposed to know?"

"How?" Frustrated beyond belief, Drew grabbed her, literally grabbed her, lifting her clean out of the chair and dragging her hard against him. "This is how!"

He crushed her mouth under his, revelling in pure sensation, ignoring her struggling, until her whole body responded avidly, angrily, full of temper and answering primitive passion.

"You *still* don't know?" Strong emotion distorted his voice. With one steely, strong movement he had her up into his arms, carrying her back through the house and up the staircase.

"Drew, put me down!" Her life had never included such galvanic action. Her whole body was shaking with anger and excitement in equal measure.

"The hell I will," he retorted. "Just shut up."

In his bedroom he threw her down on the bed, golden hair billowing, short skirt rucked up over her long exquisite legs. He grasped her wrists and pinned them to the ebony and bronze quilt. "How much punishment am I supposed to take from you?" He tried to ease his breathing but he couldn't.

"Why don't you let me go?" She tried to tug away. No hope.

"Because I love you, damn it," he gritted. "You're a woman like no other. I can't keep my hands off you. There's never been anyone else. Not Carol. *No one.* Is that what you want to hear?" Furious with her, with both of them, he lowered his head, kissing the young straining body that was arched to him. "You drive me crazy."

She felt utterly crazy, too.

There was desperation in their lovemaking that night, no gentleness, no tenderness, but a furious kind of love dance.

Drew's mouth razed her face, her throat, her body, his hands equally unappeasable, bringing her to the very edge, over and over again. All he wanted, she wanted. She wanted to cry aloud how much she loved him, how much she wanted him, but he wasn't letting her breathe.

His kisses rained down on her mouth while she lay beneath him, her breasts crushed against his chest, their flesh fused at the fulcrum.

When Eve finally convulsed, her whole body in spasm, she thought she called out to Drew. Her lover. Her soul. Only the strength of sensation was so great, the heat their bodies generated so volcanic, her lips barely moved.


When Drew drove her home much later, they were both very subdued, as though disturbed by the dark sensuality their mutual anger had unleashed. Eve's body still throbbed from that sizzling confrontation. Drew's mastery, her own high seductive power. Tonight they had entered another realm and neither could stop thinking about it.

At Eve's apartment block Drew insisted on coming in with her, waiting for her to check through the rooms. Ben hadn't come in yet. Something for once, Eve was grateful for.

"All right, I'll say goodnight." Drew nodded to her abruptly, his lean face taut. "There's something else I have to say to you, Eve. *Trust* is what relationships are built on. I can't believe you could let anything Susan could say hurt you. For the last time, Susan is my father's widow. No more. Accept that or destroy what we have."

Clearly it was an ultimatum. Though she was about to protest, say something to defend herself, Susan's behaviour was unforgivable, Drew opened the front door and strode through.

Worse, he didn't look back.


Midafternoon of the next day, still Drew hadn't called. Either it was impossible for him to find a minute off or he was totally fed up with her. Eve bowed her head at her desk and tried desperately to concentrate on her work. For reasons she couldn't explain, she felt anxiety crowding in on her other problems, an almost palpable unease. She'd already seen on television the sort of tensions that were being generated over native title. Drew himself was of the opinion everyone needed a cooling down period. But the wild card was always there. The person with the potential to incite violence. Not that Drew couldn't look after himself. He had great negotiating skills and if it ever came to a scuffle, he was superbly fit.

Around four o'clock, Jamie all but ran into her office, holding on to the doorjamb. "Eve, did you hear?" His voice was uncharacteristically sharp and loud.

"What?" She jumped up, heart lurching.

"You don't have to worry. I shouldn't have blurted it out." At her expression, Jamie tried to backtrack. "There was a news flash."

"Tell me." Eve advanced on him looking like she was ready to shake him.

"There's been some trouble at Sunderland. They don't know who's involved."

Eve almost reeled back, looking stricken. "Not Drew surely!"

"No, no, I'm sure it isn't." Jamie vigorously shook his head. But there was tension in the muscles of his face. "Drew knows how to handle himself. A vehicle has been pushed over by the crowd. There might have been anyone in it."

Eve moved back swiftly to her desk, reached into a drawer and withdrew a card. "I have Drew's mobile."

"It's not answering," Jamie told her. "Steve Holland

is already onto it. His department will follow through. We just have to wait.''

They all waited. Five o'clock came and went and no one at TCR left the building. Everyone right down to the most junior member of the staff was still haunted by the sudden death of Sir David. It was difficult indeed under the circumstances to block off the general unease. Eve, who always appeared so competent and self-contained was totally unable to hide her anxiety. Everyone felt for her.

Finally news came through which Steve Holland, top executive, took in his brusque fashion.

''Easy, easy, I'm not following you,'' he barked. ''Tell me about Forsythe. What do you mean?''

Silence while he listened. ''Well, we sure appreciate that,'' he said in an altered tone. ''I suppose we'll be seeing it tonight. Right up there on television. Many thanks. Sorry I was a bit short there but we've all been mighty anxious.''

Steve replaced the receiver. It was Eve who spoke first.

''Drew is all right?''

Steve beamed at her. ''Well, he might have a sore head for a few days, Eve. Poor old Rhys has broken his collarbone but Drew managed to deal with it. Apparently the meeting went well but they were waylaid by some hired hotheads on the way back with only one thing on their minds. *Trouble*. The driver got the wind up, tried to bulldoze through, but they rushed the car and succeeded in turning it over.

''Drew got out. Got the other two out, then took on the crowd. Whatever he had to say, it broke them up. We'll see it all tonight on television. That was Channel

Nine. Rhys has a stopover at hospital. They're flying Drew home.''

She wasn't going to wait. While staff dispersed seemingly on a high, Eve drove directly to the television station waiting for the helicopter to land. Drew was second out, his jacket folded over his arm, tieless, white shirt open at the throat. His lope was as springy as ever, limbs moving freely.

Her heart bursting with relief, Eve flew across the short distance that divided them, flinging out her arms, calling his name.

He caught her to him strongly, bent his head, kissed her mouth. ''Everything's okay, Evie.'' He felt the trembling through her. ''I'm perfectly fine.''

''But you're not!'' There was a large angry-looking graze on his right temple.

''Don't take any notice of that. It's nothing. Mindless little stunts don't do anyone any good. In fact, as far as I can make out, it worked in our favour. I believe a resolution is in sight.''

''And us?'' Eve whispered, conscious now video cameras were on them. ''I want to resolve all our differences. All I know is I'd die if I ever lost you. I love you, Drew. I can't wait to be your wife.''

It was said with such passionate intensity, Drew, despite a blinding headache, was flooded with a powerful sense of elation. Much as he had felt the love in Eve, saw it in so many ways, it was glorious to hear her put it into words.

He'd lived for this moment. This extraordinary moment.

Everyone who saw the large front page photograph of them in the morning paper, arms flung around one another, Eve's beautiful face raised to her fiancé's flashing smile, knew exactly what they were looking at. The very image of love.

Susan saw it, too. In her penthouse apartment she twisted the newspaper in her hands, her long nails unconsciously gouging holes in the page. Oh, yes, she'd stay away. A captured moment like that gave her no hope.

# CHAPTER TEN

A BRILLIANT spring afternoon.

Exquisite in her wedding raiment, Eve stood inside the Gothic doors of the packed cathedral, holding tightly to her brother's arm. The days had rushed away, now she was presenting herself to the man she so passionately loved and who loved her. Could there be a greater happiness?

Drew's pearl and diamond heart-shaped necklace lay warm against her breast. Her wedding gown of duchesse satin had the same lustre as the pearls, magnolia in colour with the faintest flush of ice green in the folds. The tiny panelled corselet bodice of her gown was strapless over the magnificent full skirt. Her short white veil caught by a high, pearl-encrusted headband had the same glimmer of ice green.

In a face made pale by deep emotion, her eyes glittered like emeralds. In her hand she carried a beautiful bouquet of all white flowers, lilies, peonies, roses, orchids, framed by delicate green foliage.

Two bridesmaids and two flower girls attended her. All in Chinese silk, their lovely dresses with billowing skirts reflecting the colours of their spring bouquets, rose-pink and lilac, mimosa yellow and a heavenly shade of blue. One of the attendants, a young girl, bore a decided resemblance to the bride, with her finely cut features, long blond hair and large, almond-shaped hazel-green eyes. A stepsister, it was later confirmed in the press, to no one's surprise.

The processional music from the great organ rang out, a wonderful composition by Handel, to thrill the soul.

Eve's walk to the flower-decked altar began.

This is my life, she thought. My life to make full and meaningful. Take hold of it.

Wedding guests turned around, smiling and exclaiming at the dazzling beauty of the bride and her procession. Some women in the beautifully dressed congregation, remembering their own wedding, had tears in their eyes.

When at last Eve reached her bridegroom, more resplendent than she had ever seen him, she saw from the brilliant glitter in his eyes he was as immensely moved as she was. This was their day. Their great celebration.

Her beloved Ben took her hand and placed it in Drew's.

"God bless you two all the days of your lives," he whispered. For a moment Ben thought he could see through time and what he saw was good.

And now the wedding ceremony began, carrying them forward on life's journey.

# In 1999 in Harlequin Romance® marriage is top of the agenda!

Get ready for a great new series by some of our most popular authors, bringing romance to the workplace! This series features gorgeous heroes and lively heroines who discover that mixing business with pleasure can lead to anything...even matrimony!

## *Books in this series are:*

January 1999
**Agenda: Attraction!** by Jessica Steele

February 1999
**Boardroom Proposal** by Margaret Way

March 1999
**Temporary Engagement** by Jessica Hart

April 1999
**Beauty and the Boss** by Lucy Gordon

May 1999
**The Boss and the Baby** by Leigh Michaels

*From boardroom...to bride and groom!*

Available wherever Harlequin books are sold.

*Makes any time special* ™

Look us up on-line at: http://www.romance.net

HRMTB

# *Harlequin Romance®*

**Rebecca Winters writes wonderful romances that pack an emotional punch you'll never forget. Brimful of brides, babies and bachelors, her new trilogy is no exception.**

Meet Annabelle, Gerard and Diana. Annabelle and Gerard are private investigators, Diana, their hardworking assistant. Each of them is about to face a rather different assignment—falling in love!

# LOVE
# undercover

*Their mission was marriage!*

Books in this series are:

**March 1999  #3545**
**UNDERCOVER FIANCÉE**

**April 1999  #3549**
**UNDERCOVER BACHELOR**

**MAY 1999  #3553**
**UNDERCOVER BABY**

Available wherever Harlequin books are sold.

## HARLEQUIN®
*Makes any time special* ™

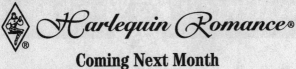

# Coming Next Month

**#3543 THE NINE-DOLLAR DADDY Day Leclaire**
Ten-year-old Hutch Lonigan had walked into the Yellow Rose Matchmakers Agency with all his savings and demanded the best man he could get for nine dollars! The sleeping partner in the family business, Ty Merrick, hadn't expected that man to be him. But one look at Cassidy Lonigan, and Ty was hearing wedding bells. Only it was going to take more than sweet talk and kisses to persuade young Hutch's stubborn mother to walk up the aisle!

**Texas Grooms Wanted!:** *Only cowboys need apply!*

**#3544 TEMPORARY ENGAGEMENT Jessica Hart**
Bubbly Flora Mason had had plans to temp and travel. Her plans had *not* included being engaged to her sexy boss, Matt Davenport. Only, Flora had needed to save face, and Matt had needed a temporary fiancée. So what if they were like chalk and cheese? It was only for two nights. But then, two nights turned into three, then four....

**Marrying the Boss:** *From boardroom to bride and groom!*

Starting next month look out for a new trilogy by bestselling author Rebecca Winters.

**#3545 UNDERCOVER FIANCÉE Rebecca Winters**
Annabelle Forrester has only ever loved one man—Rand Dumbarton. The sexy tycoon had swept her off her feet, but their whirlwind engagement had ended bitterly. She hadn't expected to have him walk back into her life and hire her! Only it seemed Rand didn't want Annabelle to work for him...he just wanted her!

**Love Undercover:** *Their mission was marriage!*

**#3546 A DAD FOR DANIEL Janelle Denison**
Tyler Whitmore had returned home after nine years to claim his half of the family business. And Brianne was right to be nervous. When Tyler had left he had taken more than her innocence—he had taken her dreams and her heart. But unbeknownst to Tyler, he had given Brianne something in return—her son, Daniel!

**BACK TO THE RANCH:** *Let Harlequin Romance® take you back to the ranch and show you how the West is won...and wooed!*